D1336625

Listen to the Children

They are ordinary people to whom something extraordinary is happening. This is the theme of a complex and most sinister mystery.

The town is Lukesfield in south-east England. Here Maggie Chase, a sensible forty-ish woman whose husband has left her, is trying to make a living with a house-cleaning business. Her small team cleans houses impartially for friend or foe, and in doing so learns quite a lot about domestic habits.

They also discover a severed hand in a cupboard.

A small boy – a boy whose uncertain mind has somehow been invaded by the fantasies of Sir James Barrie – disappears.

These events are part of a chain that leads to an epidemic in Lukesfield. Some of the people there 'developed raging symptoms, sometimes intermittent, but always strong. Such a manifestation is, medically, called florid. These unlucky ones had a full, fine, flowered illness.'

Maggie has a boyfriend, a policeman. This relationship is to prove both a complication and in some ways a help as Maggie feels compelled to search for the missing boy, Sam.

Here the children are portrayed as a separate, dangerous species: savage little animals with their own weird groupings and rituals.

It is a story full of fascination and foreboding in which the solution to the mystery is approached by mundane common-sense on the one hand and on the other by the free range of the imagination.

by the same author

COME HOME AND BE KILLED
BURNING IS A SUBSTITUTE FOR LOVING
THE HUNTER IN THE SHADOWS
NUN'S CASTLE
IRONWOOD
RAVEN'S FORGE
DRAGON'S EYE
AXWATER
MURDER HAS A PRETTY FACE
THE PAINTED CASTLE
THE HAND OF GLASS

LISTEN TO THE CHILDREN

Jennie Melville

First published in Great Britain 1986 by
MACMILLAN LONDON LIMITED
4 Little Essex Street London WC2R 3LF and Basingstoke

Associated companies in Auckland, Delhi, Dublin, Gaborone, Hamburg, Harare, Hong Kong, Johannesburg, Kuala Lumpur, Lagos, Manzini, Melbourne, Mexico City, Nairobi, New York, Singapore and Tokyo

Typeset by Bookworm Typesetting Ltd

Printed by Anchor Brendon Ltd.

Extracts from *Peter Pan* and *Margaret Ogilvy* by J.M. Barrie reprinted by permission of Hodder and Stoughton Limited.

British Library Cataloguing in Publication Data

Melville, Jennie
Listen to the children.
I. Title
823′.914[F] PR6063.E44

ISBN 0-333-40767-9

Chapter One

November 1st. Post Hallowe'en.

Libraries are dangerous places. No one knows how dangerous. Perhaps because books are made from paper and paper is made from trees and some trees are dangerous.

Maggie Chase, on her way to pick up the latest Dick Francis and hide from her creditors, was knocked against the wall by a swarm of small, violent departing children. She leaned against the wall, dazzled by a sudden image of small feet pushing through a bloody stream. Or a stream of blood. It glistened.

In that stream of blood small fish like objects surged and glistened, things with big heads and tadpole bodies. They were like tiny little human foetuses, newly conceived, being flushed along in blood. Children not yet born, or never to be born.

A sharp breath and it was gone. This was the first episode of its kind.

Herself again, she recognised the children to be in the yellow, brown and white of Miss Pettit's School, in other words privileged kids in a hurry. The fees at Pettit's were known to be high. Behind the children hurried Biddy Powell, the present headmistress of the school, and also its part-owner, although Miss Pettit herself was alive and omnipresent. Biddy almost knocked Maggie over again, stopping herself just in time. She apologised and picked up Maggie's books.

'Sorry, Maggie. They've got the devil in their tails I'm afraid, little wretches, I hoped the library would calm them down but it doesn't seem to have worked that way. They've been wild all day. . . . I try to show them how a library works and let them choose books.'

'How often do you come?' Maggie thought they had sped out more like wild beasts on the hunt than children about to have a quiet read, but then she was always cautious with children. It paid in her opinion.

'It varies. About twice a term.' Biddy's tone was apologetic, she guessed that Maggie would avoid these times in future if she could. 'See you soon. Come and have a meal. You're looking better.'

Even tactful, kind Biddy (with troubles of her own to illuminate her mind) said things like that, which made Maggie want to bare her teeth. She did not want to look 'better' because that implied she had looked worse.

After this little episode Maggie chose a cookery book to read in bed. She could not afford to do luxury cooking nor had she anyone to share her bed, so it was all vicarious pleasures and here cookery seemed a safer bet than sex. She wondered briefly what Miss Lavender, the librarian, would have said if she had asked for the *Kama Sutra* or *The Murderer's Encyclopaedia*? Nothing probably, but put on her usual poker face.

How are things, Maggie? she asked herself as she let herself into her house. Not good. No hope of your marriage surviving. He's gone, hasn't he? So if no one else will say it: I will say it for you. What did you do wrong, Maggie? One day you will know the answer.

April 1st

Five months later Maggie did not know any more answers but was much more self-confident. She had survived both the departure of her husband and the loss of her job as manageress of the local dress and lingerie shop. She had started her own business and was now the inventor and sole owner of High-Lo Cleaners, which undertook the cleaning of houses from top to bottom in the prosperous district of Lukesfield where she lived. You had to be prosperous to pay Maggie's price.

It was while pursuing her new career that the discovery of the hand was made.

Maggie Chase and Evadne Rhys were cleaning a house which was about to be sold. Cleaning it professionally from top to bottom. Work had not been very plentiful these last weeks in Lukesfield. Circumstances there had been a little peculiar lately to say the least. The disappearance of a strange but beautiful child, an atmosphere of bloody decay and death, these things had fallen on Lukesfield like a disease.

Certain forms of death distance domestic routines. People don't think of cleaning and painting at such a time. Then, suddenly, work flooded in again. Everyone wanted to be cleaned. This old house called Gavelkind was high on their list of houses needing their attention. It belonged to the elderly aunt of a local dentist.

They had come to the house together in Maggie's old car. Evadne was cleaning a deep cupboard when she drew back with a scream.

'There's a hand in the cupboard.'

Maggie tried for a black joke. 'Don't shake it then,' and went to take a look. She had been under a lot of pressure lately.

'It's a human hand,' said Evadne unsteadily, and fainted.

It was when she saw the bloody hand that Maggie began to realise what had befallen her. Not the murder mystery of the century (as one newspaper had put it) but something stranger, wilder and more Brontëan.

She might die herself. Others certainly would, some already had. That was what the hand was signalling: shake me, those who are about to die. By creating fantasies in her own mind, Maggie had helped create murder.

As they had arrived at the house Maggie had said, 'I might be getting married again.' She was tall, blonde and capable, sometimes cool, sometimes warm and impulsive, always good-hearted.

'Oh, I'm so glad.' Evadne, happily married herself, liked to feel it was the same for her friend. 'David, I suppose?'

'I think it will be David,' said Maggie as if she had a choice. Evadne's nose wrinkled with interest. Goodness, she thought, perhaps it's that *other* one.

Maggie had spoken simply and shyly, and not unhappily. But not happily either. People who were close to recent events in which death and violence came were cautious about being happy in Lukesfield just now, it seemed to tempt providence. 'I have to get a divorce of course. But at least I know where my husband is now.' He had gone away, without a word, some eighteen months ago. 'He agrees to a divorce.' She grinned suddenly. 'Mind you, with all that's been happening in Lukesfield perhaps I should not count on too much.'

Maggie was thin and tense, not ready yet to relax. So much of the story was still untold, some of it her own story. She had the uneasy feeling that she might never get to know it herself. Her life might go on yet she would be lost in a cloud of unknowing. The concept alarmed her, as well it might. She put it down to fatigue.

Evadne, being less imaginative, and also less involved in what had been going on in Lukesfield, bore the shadow of her own future more lightly.

They had settled beforehand that Maggie would clean downstairs while Evadne did upstairs, but when they got inside Gavelkind they stayed together, tacitly admitting that they did not like this house.

'Who's it sold to, do you know?' asked Evadne.

'A medical man. Specialises in mental health. Same outfit as bought the Wylies' house. He's coming ahead.'

He was the forerunner of a crowd, coming ahead to set things up.

'Ah.' Evadne took the information in without comment. 'Remember when we cleaned Oakwood?'

Maggie remembered.

They cleaned downstairs speedily, then went upstairs together. Thus they were in the same room when Evadne found the hand.

But this terrible discovery in the house of Arthur Chamberlain's aunt was not the beginning of the Lukesfield story. Rather it was two stops from the end. For the two women it had begun much earlier.

Lukesfield was a Kentish village, far south of London. Places have a history and a character sometimes before they have a name. In any case the name should always be taken into account.

This place, where the events happened, was called, angelically, St Lukes Field. Latterly the saint was dropped from the name and it became Lukesfield, a wealthy commuter district with large houses set in landscaped gardens. Lukesfield lay in the path of strong acid-bearing winds seeded by the industrial belt to the north. At the heart of the community was a worked-out gravel pit surrounded by stunted trees and scrub, and dominated by one large spreading oak which seemed to have a source of water and nourishment all its own. This was an area of twenty acres of long-disused gravel pits, dug out of ancient woodland. Time had filled in some of the pits, left others as small ponds and muddy pools, marshy fringed. Trees. One great oak seemed to prosper heartily, however; perhaps it had deeper roots than its peers, or thrived on challenge, or did better with dead rivals. During this period of ten years there was a Year of the Tree, but this tree did very well on its own, thank you. One day this vacant ground of the gravel pits was to be a country club, or a pleasure centre with boats, or a nine-hole golf course. It all waited on the whim of the right developer, who hadn't yet appeared. Until that happened it was a playground for dogs and children. House-agents in the neighbourhood used this as a selling-point, praising it as being so marvellous for children, especially for those houses whose gardens abutted on the gravel pits. Pettit's School was such a house, also the Wylies' home and Maggie Chase's smaller villa. All this gravel-pit area belonged to old Mr Curzon whose family had once owned the whole of Lukesfield, but who now lived in London and never came near the place. No one knew him. Miss Pettit remembered him as a boy whom she had taught. In which case, if Mr Curzon was old then Miss Pettit must be even older since she had instructed him. She was old, no doubt about that, and only mentioned Tommy Curzon with pursed lips. He had been a handful.

After the terrible things happened in Lukesfield the lives of some people lost their bloom just like the trees, some to recover, others not.

The names of Maggie Chase, Mary Powell and Ellen and Sam Wylie come to mind. Also two professionals: Charley Soul and Joe Archibald. The one believed in the death of the world; the other was the journalist also interested in ecology. Also Miss Catriona Mackenzie, who lived unnaturally because she had outlived her child. This opened paths in her mind wonderfully. It also inclined her to think of children, not necessarily with love, but with an understanding that they were not tiny adults as in a Velasquez painting, but another species with their own rules. Among the dramatis personae, were two from the past, proving that it does not die. One was a young housewife with flaming red hair and an arrogance of soul to match. Proud and wilful unto death, screaming abuse in her death agonies. Also a small man, a head too big for his boots with a rounded forehead, pouched sad eyes, and a moustache. He had delicate hands, feet somewhat too large for him, but shod in Piccadilly. A man who had suffered all his life for a dead brother. Both these people from the past.

In this district circles mixed and matched. You met your dentist at the Local History Group, the librarian at the Oxfam coffee morning, and met a man from the local newspaper at Chapel. Things get known, who drinks, whose wife is leaving him, where the new road will go, where the new mental hospital will be sited on what rough piece of ground.

Maggie Chase, when this point was put to her, called it simplistic, which it was for people and vegetables alike, for so many other factors entered in.

At about this time a marketing campaign for a new kitchen cleaner called Flight was launched. It had been intended originally to test-market it in a small Scottish town called Bardin Links, but a suspected outbreak of foot-and-mouth disease on two farms there meant that an order discouraging unnecessary movement of motor vehicles in Bardin Links went into force. So the test-marketing of Flight was switched to Lukesfield. A box of Flight was deposited on every step, free. No one was forgotten, not the Wylies, not Pettit's School, nor Maggie. The dentist got two, one at his surgery and the other at home. Even Joe Archibald in his caravan received his gift, and Charley Soul would have done also had he so desired it, and made his presence felt.

The advertising agency which had evolved the packaging and

the name of the product had wished to call it Flite, but the inventor was a reader of Dickens, and, in honour of Miss Flite, had decreed the straightforward spelling of the goods. He died within the year. Not too soon to learn the use that his product was put to in Lukesfield.

In the skies above the little town an American satellite swung in orbit; not far away a Russian capsule circled. Each had their appointed time above Lukesfield. The people below were not conscious of them, although they were aware that space above them was no longer empty. Almost every day they heard reports of some new objects sent up to circulate.

One man, though, thought of the satellites with interest, with hope, and sometimes with fear. He was a devout man who understood that he was in touch with the spirit world, and it might be that the satellites could help in his mission of telling the world. 'God wishes us to make use of natural science,' he said in his preaching, honestly and perhaps truly. They must use all the Power there was around.

Charley Soul. It was an adopted name used for what he called professional purposes. He went where he was welcome which was not everywhere. He was in the long tradition of itinerant preachers, a latter-day Bible Man, although he had not been born to the task but self-converted after a death in the family.

Death was always with him now. 'It is not our life but our death that is Providence's great gift to use, it renews the world,' he preached. 'Faith is a hurdle. Leap over it and you will be in the kingdom.' But he knew it was hard to jump.

There was no call to celibacy in his preaching, indeed he liked women and, quite often, they liked him. He had noticed at least two women in Lukesfield who attracted him. One had only to remember that the relationship was in the hands of Providence and not to exceed natural laws. That kept you all right and well away from eternal punishment. He was, and knew himself to be, a bit two-faced.

He rubbed his cheek; his sinus was playing him up. But he would be getting treatment for it. One good thing. He had not done well in Lukesfield, the wrong district perhaps, although the area had a long history of nonconformity, and before that of extreme Puritanism. But that was in the past, those old-rooted families had either died or moved away; the newcomers were different.

He had held regular meetings in the Free Bible Hall, preaching with more than usual force, yet few had followed him as pilgrims. They were a godless lot round here. One open air meeting, in the area where the gravel pits had once been, had been unpleasant, even dangerous since a small fire had broken out in a bush.

All the same, he was a sensitive man, used to assessing the atmosphere, playing to the audience as it were, and he felt *something* in Lukesfield, some spiritual force which was reaching out to him.

The moment he felt this he should have gone away from Lukesfield, well away.

There were always to be two views about the events that took place over the next months. Was it straightforwardly criminous? Thus adequately explained by psychological stresses and emotional miseries, or even downright wickedness? Or was there another, more alarming explanation? One which postulates a process which might go on and on?

Maggie was always grateful that she kept an open mind, even when her own sanity was called in question.

She was enjoying her new beginning; she like being her own boss. Not much money in it yet, but only three months and she was very nearly into profit.

She was thinking about this one morning as she prepared for work. Happy dreams. Unaware that from that moment on she was about to step into a nightmare world. A series of events in which the finding of the hand would be among the most hideous, but not the worst, nor the last.

'Think the police will stop us as suspicious characters? They've been very much on the alert lately. We are in what they call the "new wave crime belt".'

Lukesfield invited burglaries with its opulent open-plan houses, many Rolls and Mercedes, and general air of having an emerald-studded Longines watch on every dressing-table.

Evadne was speaking, a sturdy young woman wearing jeans,

a heavy-duty sweater, and a silk headscarf of surprising beauty. This was a necessary symbol of her position as a well-off young wife who just worked because she liked to. Her husband had insisted on it. She was standing by an aged Volvo which was loaded to the roof with two vacuum cleaners, an automatic carpet-cleaner, three mops, several buckets and an assortment of bottles, sprays and tins of polishes. A large ladder was superimposed on all this, tied on insecurely with rope. This was the High-Lo Cleaners circus about to get on the road.

The bonnet of the Volvo was open and Maggie was peering into it.

'What's that? Why? Why should the police be after us? This rotten oil gauge never tells the truth. . . . I should think the police have better things to do than worry about us. . . . Hand me that screwdriver, Evadne.'

'The ladder . . . we might be planning a break-in.'

'With Sophy and Elspeth aiding and assisting? Where are they by the way? Late again? No, don't tell me.' Maggie lowered the bonnet. 'When I can afford it I will buy us a lovely new van with HIGH-LO CLEANERS on it in large letters. A white van, I think, to show what a good job we do.' She was off on a dream again.

'You certainly need a new van. We won't seize up at the Pilling roundabout again, will we? Not like last time. I was late back to tea and it makes Steve so cross if I'm late.'

'He likes you to earn, doesn't he?'

'Oh yes, but he likes his meals on time too.' Evadne was an anxious wife. She thought if Maggie had been a little more anxious she might have had her husband still.

'Well, I'll try to avoid the Pilling roundabout if I can this time. It was a little public.' Quite a crowd had gathered, and Evadne's husband had *seen.* A total mistake. Steve did not like his wife talked about, let alone noticed. 'I've spoken to the engine and it's promised.'

Evadne still looked apprehensive. Once again Maggie accepted her aide's total lack of humour. Or perhaps it was just Maggie's jokes that did not appeal. Since Maggie had only just got back to making jokes of any sort, this seemed a shame.

'Where are the girls?'

'Already in the car.'

'I couldn't see them when I looked.'

'They are behind the Hoover. Elspeth is holding it.'

It was the biggest machine available. The girls, two fragile-looking *élégantes* in pretty pastel jeans, peered around the obstruction and waved.

They won't last, thought Maggie. Their nail varnish will chip, and I will never see them again. In this she was to find herself wrong.

Life with Maggie's team could be rough, tough and hard, as she would have been the first to admit. Was the first to admit, said it aloud often, although not when anyone was listening. She had started High-Lo Cleaners for strictly financial reasons. She had a home, hands and the need to earn. So she had had her good idea and invented her home cleaners. She and her band went from house to house in the prosperous district around them, charging high prices but doing a good job. The fact that she had once worked in the local lingerie shop meant that every woman in the neighbourhood knew and trusted her. She found herself enjoying her new way of life. Fitting underclothes had provided surprising insights into other people's lives ('You'd be surprised what some people wear under a Ted Lapidus model'), but her new work was teaching her a lot more. For instance, who would have thought that old Mrs Buchanan had a fetish about boots? Well, anyway she had three dozen pairs, all unworn. Or that anyone still used chamberpots!

'Who needs a husband when they've got High-Lo Cleaners?' Maggie asked herself, as she got into her car. For a moment her shoulders sagged. She did miss Christopher, some days worse than others. Did he miss her? How would she ever know? Some day she would understand why he had gone, but this was not that day. Life had somehow removed Christopher and produced David in his place as a surprise bundle, although exactly what was wrapped up in that bundle remained to be seen. She put the thought of David aside and started up the car, which came to life with its usual jerk, but did agree to start. It had been ill-used in its time, that car, and it showed. Like me, Maggie thought, but self-pity was not her style so she set that aside and put her foot down.

A double scream from behind told her that Sophy and Elspeth had felt the start. One usually did when Maggie drove. It was one of the many skills she had mastered but never quite perfected. Living itself, she suspected, was another of them. But I'm learning, she told herself. I picked myself up this time and went on. Next time I shall do better.

'Hang on, girls, we're off.' With another jerk, they were.

Soon they were passing Miss Pettit's School where the children were just running into the playground, wild as ever.

'Like a pack of hungry wolves,' Maggie observed absently, turning her head away. 'Nothing innocent about that lot.'

'They haven't actually eaten anyone, have they?' Evadne had a child herself, one not yet able to walk, whom she was thinking of sending to Miss Pettit's if they could afford the fees. To earn the fees was one of the reasons why she was working. It was important to give your child a good start in life. And Pettit's did that for you. Your offspring mixed with the *right* sort of children. She wasn't going to stand for Maggie's black jokes.

'We're cleaning there on Thursday so we can find out. But don't worry, we are taking John Henry to protect us.'

'I love John Henry,' said Sophy enthusiastically from the back.

'Don't we all?'

John Henry was a young actor who worked for Maggie when 'resting' from the stage, which was almost always. He introduced himself modestly as 'only a hoofer', but inside himself he thought he might one day be as good as Olivier. If only he could get the parts. He was very butch on the outside and much much less butch inside. Maggie was very well aware of all these nuances, but, no sexist, she employed him because he was a good, willing worker, and there was no denying that a man's strength and a man's presence were sometimes very useful.

'Do we need him for protection?' Evadne was startled.

'Joke,' said Maggie, unwilling to let Evadne into the precise nature of her unease about the school. She was reluctant, for that matter, to admit it to herself. It was uncomfortable to associate images of blood with young children. She wished that this sense of blood as unguent clinging to the children would go away. But it had persisted since the episode at the library. She blamed herself. She ought to have forgotten all about it. She hoped she wasn't turning into an obsessive person.

But Evadne walked right into her thoughts. As she was apt to do. It was not sensitivity. Evadne was not sensitive, except to child and husband where she was all quivering antennae. No, it was a well-developed knack of knowing where the action was going, like a good journalist.

'They've been very jumpy there since that Hallowe'en party, I've heard.' Evadne's tone was very judicial. 'We'll never get to the bottom of what went wrong there.'

'Well, you can ask Ellen Wylie for yourself.' Maggie was turning neatly, for her, into the drive of the Wylie house. 'She was the one who gave the party.'

And it had been another nail in Ellen Wylie's reputation, which was not too good at the best of times. She drank too much, they said. A lazy mother. Not much of a housekeeper, either. A beautiful woman, though. But no wonder her husband wanted out. All the sympathies were with Nicholas.

Nicholas was the reason High-Lo had this job. The divorce he wanted was being arranged, and as part of the deal this house was being sold. To Ellen's fury, it was said. Since Ellen claimed she had done no housework since the divorce was bruited (and precious little before, said the neighbours), Nick had arranged for High-Lo to do a professional job. At the price he meant to get, buyers would expect to see clean paint, walls, carpets and curtains. He hated doing this to Ellen, putting her to shame, but there was a sort of hard clarity inside Nicholas that made him see what he had to do and push his point through even while he hurt. There was a lot of pain floating around the Wylie household and he had his share of it. Guilt, too.

Ellen did not answer Maggie's ring at the bell, or make any move to let the High-Lo team in, although she was expecting them and had agreed to both day and time of arrival. Maggie herself had confirmed arrangements on the telephone the day before. No matter. Maggie raised an eyebrow, pushed open the door, which was not locked, and waved the girls in. 'Enter, ladies. Make yourselves comfortable and then unload the van. I'll look for Ellen.'

The girls scrambled out. If they were reluctant they were carefully not showing it. No one was admitting to a certain unwillingness to begin the cleaning of this particular establishment.

'Six bedrooms,' said Sophy to Elspeth. 'At least.' And every last one of them dirty.

The Wylie house – mansion, Maggie called it to herself – was large, modern, avant-garde in design and planned to be easy to run. The many rooms were well shaped, the wooden staircase and doors of pale and gleaming satinwood, and the floors close and thickly carpeted. The only exception was the room Nicholas called his study, where an antique French carpet rested on a floor of true herring-bone parquetry. Nicholas loved old craft-made objects. All over the house and especially in the kitchen his collection of ancient household apparatus was spread out. Perhaps Ellen had a point in resenting it. She did resent it. Nicholas's toys, as she called them mockingly, were one of the dividers of their marriage, just as her mess of cosmetics in the bathroom and bedroom was her offering on the pyre.

Pre-eminently, Oakwood needed to be immaculate, and this it was not. Sticky fingers had planted jam and worse on the pale wood, dirty feet had marched boldly across the velvet carpets leaving defiant trails, grease had splashed the silk of the upholstery: if Ellen had noticed she had done nothing about it.

Now Maggie's team were moving in to do what they could. It was a house with a strange atmosphere, Maggie had to admit, and might not be too responsive to a clean. Perhaps it was one of those houses that liked to look bedraggled, like some women. A kind of drop-out house.

'No sign of our charming hostess.'

'She's in the garden,' said Evadne. 'She always is. Acting like a bird.'

She pointed through the kitchen window to where a figure could be seen stretched out in a hammock with a glass in one hand and a cigarette in the other. 'Only birds don't drink and smoke so much.'

'The house stinks of smoke,' said Sophy, wrinkling her nose.

Smoke mixed with Guerlain, one had to be fair to Ellen. Chamade really smelt good when mixed with cigarettes, it intensified the effect, made it very sexy. And come to think of it, that was what Ellen was all about, and what the neighbourhood had against her. Sex rampant. She had been a successful young actress once, and Lukesfield held it against her, not that she was, but that she had given it up. A star, seen on TV or on the London stage, would have been a nice thing for Lukesfield to have. They would have loved to have been connected with a series, a nice long-playing one. Ellen had been in a series once, one about a doctor. But that had been in the days Ellen called BS. Before Sam.

But there was another smell too, and Maggie wondered if she was the only one who smelt it. One of Maggie's imaginings.

It was a stink really. She borrowed Sophy's word. Stale blood.

Then she realised that Evadne's nose was wrinkling as well. Not imagination then.

On the table was a strongly wrapped brown paper parcel. It looked as though it had been there for a day or two, growing into the table with odd bits of newspaper, apple peel and spent matches sprouting upon it.

A label said: 'Wylie, Oakwood, Lukesfield, Kent. Venison sent express from Exmoor.'

'Hasn't she heard of refrigeration?' whispered Sophy.

Maggie touched the parcel: it was stuck to the table. The smell seemed to grow stronger as if taking life from her touch.

She drew back. 'Evadne, Sophy, you start work on the kitchen.'

'Oh lovely.' Evadne looked at the grease on the floor.

'Elspeth, get the things out of the car. . . . I'll go and talk to Ellen.' That woman would give them at least a word if it had to be dragged out of her.

The telephone rang as Maggie went through the hall; she hesitated, then picked it up.

'Hi, Bunty,' said a confident male voice, before she could

utter. 'Is Bunty-girl there?'

'This is the Wylie house,' returned Maggie sedately. 'Hold on, please, I'll see if she's here.'

Carrying the telephone, which was fortunately the cordless type, she advanced towards the figure in the garden.

As she walked across the sunlit garden towards Ellen, who was not looking her way, she could hear the self-assured baritone chirruping away down below.

Ellen opened one sapphire-blue eye. She was a lovely young woman wrecking her looks with self-abuse. Maggie, who was very nice to look at herself, enjoyed Ellen's looks and deplored what she was doing to them.

Maggie pushed the telephone over to Ellen. 'Here. Someone wants Bunty.'

Ellen stared at her, with expressionless blue eyes, apparently not even seeing her. Nevertheless, she reached out a languid hand and took the telephone.

'Bunty doesn't live here any more,' she said to the telephone, banging the receiver down on the cheerful baritone, thus cutting it off in mid voice.

Lucky Bunty, thought Maggie. She was right to move out.

'There's a joint of meat rotting away on the kitchen table,' she said. Having said it, she felt, somehow, as if it was her doing, and that it was a leg or an arm of hers that was wrapped up and quietly decaying in brown paper.

She swallowed.

Ellen handed her back the telephone graciously, like a queen giving away a prize. She was pretty drunk.

'That's Nicky's meat. It belongs to my husband. He ordered it. A standing order of a joint once a month. I can't stop it coming. Keeps on and on coming. Let him deal with it.'

Behind Ellen was a rose garden, in the depths of which Maggie could see a child running about. One of the Wylie brood, no doubt. There were two boys.

'Aren't they at school?'

'Just Sam. He didn't feel well.' Ellen was defensive.

Maggie nodded. She knew about Sam, and guessed that Sam was about fifty per cent the cause of the break-up of the Wylies' marriage. The rest was forty-five per cent Ellen all on her own.

'I'll put the meat away somewhere, and perhaps you could tell Nicholas what he has to deal with.' Her tone was unconsciously grim.

'He can give it away to Biddy Powell. She's the bitch he's leaving me for. You know that, of course. Everyone knows everything round here. Let her have the meat.'

Maggie kept quiet. She knew Biddy was in love with Nicholas, it had showed for years, long before he had noticed it. Biddy was a good sort, she liked her, pity to wish the meat on her. Still, you take Nicholas, you take his meat, obviously.

Sam came running out of the rose garden to stand by his mother. He was a slender pale-skinned child of about eight years. Sometimes he looked immeasurably older, with a little pinched elderly face under flaxen curls. Other times, he looked as young and innocent as a Donatello cherub. Today was Italian Renaissance day.

He didn't look ill, and he did not speak. As far as Maggie knew, he never spoke.

This did not mean he did not communicate, because when he desired to do so, he jolly well did. It was because she knew this fact that Maggie always sided with those who said his mind was all right, if you could only get through to it. Speech was just not his medium.

Ellen put an arm protectively around him. Somewhere, somehow, inside this changeling of mine, her look said, is a good, clever, wise child, all locked in. Autistic, they called it.

Suddenly, Maggie saw a great red, bloody snake like an umbilical cord stretching between Sam and his mother. The snake seemed to wind its way past them both down the garden, out past the garage and into the road. She closed her eyes, but there it still was, imprinted on her inner vision, as a glistening tube of blood.

Of course there was nothing to be seen. Never had been, one must believe, or the rules of nature were violated.

I wonder if I've got migraine, she thought, and this is how it takes me?

Neither Sam nor Ellen gave any appearance of having noticed

anything wrong with her, so perhaps she had showed nothing. Sam was a professional non-noticer, of course.

Ellen swung Sam round so that he faced her with his back towards Maggie; she bent her head towards him. Her lips moved. No sound came from her son, but there was no doubt that a conversation of some sort was going on. Ellen got up and started to lead her son into the house, Sam suddenly looking more of a little old man. He really might be ill from that face which had arrived on him so suddenly.

Maggie followed them in.

'There's been a lot of shit going round that bloody school for weeks,' said Ellen over her shoulder. The freedom of her launguage was another thing the neighbours had against Ellen. She had her friends, of course, who enjoyed her racy vitality, but as this was now at a low ebb even these friends seemed to have melted away. Fair weather friends were worse than Ellen deserved, but what she got.

'Ah,' said Maggie thoughtfully.

Ellen turned round at once. 'I know what you mean by that Ah. You mean that it's not the bloody school that's the trouble but my bloody Hallowe'en party. I know what people are saying: that the kids have been sick ever since.'

'Not sick.'

'Jumpy then. Odd. Peculiar and not funny peculiar. Not that I believe them. Most of the kids look pretty normal to me. And if they're not then it's their parents' fault, not mine. What did I do? I tried to give them a decent party, that's what I tried to do. And do I get any thanks for it? No. I'm declared guilty without a chance to plead innocence. I've got to be guilty of something in this rotten place. . . . I thought better of you, Maggie.'

Maggie moved a step away from such bitterness. 'I don't know anything about the party,' she said firmly. 'The Ah was only a noise. I was clearing my throat.'

Ellen gave her the baffled look of one who is for ever being stunned and surprised by her bad luck, and led Sam into the house. 'If you say so. But from where I stand it looks like someone hates me. Everyone probably. I'm Lukesfield's least popular lady.'

And she was exactly right. In the eyes of Lukesfield Ellen had nothing to be said for her. It was a pity she knew it so clearly because it did not help her to behave well. Maggie knew all about that feeling of anger.

Ellen took her son into the ground-floor washroom and Maggie went into the kitchen which already smelt sweeter. 'What happened to the meat?'

Evadne explained, 'I found an old-fashioned meat-safe outside, part of Nick's collection, I suppose. He's got an old coffee-grinder, a cast iron meat-mincer, and a terrible old cheese board with a wire cutter. Ghastly. I threw them out with the meat-safe. Anyway, it said Game-safe on it in large letters, so venison being game I popped it inside. I didn't think he'd mind.'

'The flies will get at it.'

'So they will,' said Evadne pleasantly, 'and good luck to them.'

Maggie put her head out of the back door and took a quick look in the yard by the garage, then she drew it in quickly. Judging by what she could see the flies had already found it. Their steady hum was an unpleasant accompaniment to the day. Why should the hum of flies be so unpleasing? Because you knew what flies did? Laid eggs from which maggots came forth ready to eat that on which they were laid.

'Know anyone called Bunty?' she asked Evadne as she turned round.

Evadne said not, but it was probably a play name of Ellen's. She had several. It was supposed to hide her casual infidelities from Nick, but naturally did not.

Ellen came out of the lavatory, leading Sam looking like a betrayed little animal. So did Ellen for that matter. The family resemblance was very strong that morning as they both went into the garden.

'Think she heard?' said Evadne

Maggie shrugged; she thought that Ellen had.

'Isn't she going to help us at all?'

'No. Leave her alone. She's in trouble.'

'Be practical, Maggie. She's always in trouble. She is trouble. I'm totally on Nick's side.'

As everyone was in Lukesfield. For a sophisticated community their view of the Wylies' marriage was surprisingly simplistic: Nicholas was a splendid young man at the top of his professional ladder (he was a lawyer), while Ellen was a bad wife and a worse mother. Biddy Powell, who impinged on the situation, was seen as a redeemer figure, saving Nicholas from a terrible life. There must be something in the characters of all three that summoned up such open judgements. Perhaps all three were a little larger than life. Maggie agreed with almost everything that was said on the subject but with the difference that she had a sneaking affection for Ellen. Biddy she had known for years and found maddeningly likeable, you had to like Biddy, but bad girl Ellen was really her favourite.

The High-Lo crew worked hard for the next few hours. Ellen had not lied when she had claimed that she had done no housework since Nicholas had announced his love for Biddy Powell. She might have gone further and said that she had lain in wait for him to be unfaithful and had put down a store of dirty dishes, unwashed linen and unswept floors like a bride building up a dowry. It was hard for Maggie and the girls to believe that what they had was only a few weeks' dirt. It looked more like a life's legacy.

They piled broken kitchen dishes into boxes, added the great variety of burnt saucepans that Ellen had produced, and piled on top the many empty tins that were stowed away at odd points around the floor. There were too many bottles to count so they had a box to themselves. Milk bottles were another silent army to be washed and then set by the back door for the milkman to collect.

Maggie put them out herself. The flies were still at it.

All this time Ellen did not come into the house, but sat under the tree where Sam occasionally visited her.

'Don't you think it odd?' asked Evadne. 'Here's this child supposed to be ill and yet there he is in the garden. I know it's sunny but it's not that warm. Why doesn't she bring him into the house?'

'Just likes the outside, I suppose.' But it was odd and Maggie knew it was odd. There was a great unease around, which she thought stemmed from Ellen. She wasn't happy in her skin, that girl, let alone her house.

They worked on, taking a picnic lunch. Several times the telephone rang, but they were straightforward calls, none of which Ellen answered, anyway. No one else wanted Bunty.

At three o'clock the school bus, driven by Biddy Powell's assistant, stopped outside, two children jumped out and with a hoot the bus drove on. For all the notice that Ellen took the hoot need not have been given. But Maggie heard and looked out.

The children, a boy and a girl, ran round the side of the house to the garden. They did it as if this was something they did every day together. They were holding hands.

Maggie was surprised. The boy was Tom Wylie (and it was ridiculous how like to Nick he was, a pocket edition of his stocky father, whereas Sam was *quite* different), but the girl was Mary Powell, the last child she would have expected to come dancing into Ellen's garden with an 'I am welcome' look all over her face.

Children, of course, were unpredictable and you must expect their friendship to light where it would, but what about Biddy? Her part in this was questionable. Was she promoting the friendship for some motive of her own? She could be, since she knew how Nicholas adored his elder son and mirror image. Even good-lady Biddy might have her calculations.

Maggie waited to see the children approach Ellen, almost expecting a cry of rage from that perverse lady or else a cold turning away. But Tom threw his arms round his mother and kissed her, then Mary did the same. It was true that Ellen was more kissed than kissing, but the event took place. Then Sam came in for his share and there were more kisses and hugs all round.

Evadne looked over her shoulder. 'Poor children. So innocent. It's a pity they have to learn what the world's about. This lot doesn't know what's going on, do they?'

Maggie turned away. 'I think they do.' She didn't know how she knew that, but she did know it. 'But never mind. How are the bedrooms going? Nearly through?'

Evadne took the hint. 'Yes, nearly done. 'I'm running back

up. I just have to polish the window. That's what I came down for. Need a clean duster. ... Sophy and Elspeth are just rehanging the curtains. By rights, *they* should go to the laundry, but we've brushed them down and sponged out the worst of the spots. Sophy is very neat-fingered. Elspeth did a very good job on the bathroom carpet. ... Blood, I think that was, but she reduced it. You never get rid of blood.'

'No,' agreed Maggie. 'Blood does hang around.' In the mind as well as on the ground. No more of that, Maggie, she commanded.

'Those two have done well today,' went on Evadne judicially. 'I must admit I never thought they'd stick it out. Be gone by midday, I said. But no, they showed up to be really good workers. I had to instruct them a bit at first. This and that, you know, you could tell they've never really done much of this sort of work. But they've soon caught on. They've done well.'

'We all have. God, I'm tired,' Maggie yawned. She had slept badly the night before which was not surprising in all the circumstances that surrounded her.

The noise of the children filtered into the house. From the sounds that Maggie heard she guessed that they were playing a version of Mothers and Fathers with a dash of Peter Pan. 'I'm Wendy and this is my house,' she heard Mary call out. 'You can be Peter and he's Tinkerbell.'

She went to the garden door to take a look at this house. Tom-Peter was still building it from branches of trees; he was about to roof it with an old umbrella. Mary-Wendy was stocking her kitchen with broken bits of pots. So they had been rooting away in the rubbish thrown out from the kitchen. It was to be hoped they hadn't interfered with the meat-safe.

The children saw her looking and stopped their game. A silence fell. It was up to Maggie to break it if anyone did.

'Why is he Tinkerbell?' she heard herself ask.

Mary-Wendy looked thoughtful. What to say to this strange human animal whom I do not know, she seemed to be asking herself. This was unfair, because she did know Maggie.

'Because he can fly,' she answered at last.

There was no answer to that except to say show me but it was undignified bandying words with a child just because she had put you down. Besides, it might turn out that Sam could fly, and if so Maggie did not want to see it.

She withdrew to the house. 'Stay away from the meat-safe,' she said.

By five o'clock they were packing to go.

'Cuppa?' Evadne was already putting on the kettle. Usually they did not poach on an employer's food or heat, but everyone felt Ellen owed them something.

Maggie nodded. 'Yes, and take one out to Ellen. I want her cheque for the bill. Or cash if possible.' She was sitting at the kitchen table, now immaculate, making out the account. It was going to be higher then she'd estimated for, but that was Ellen's fault. The more the dirt, the more you paid.

Evadne rolled her eyes sceptically as she departed with the mug of tea. She had a gift for pulling faces, all without showing a scrap of humour. More as if her face was elastic and she liked occasionally to give it a tug.

Maggie waited. Sophy and Elspeth were packing away the equipment in the car. She was alone in the kitchen.

Tired, but satisfied with the day's work, she moved to the door and stood there breathing in the soft air while she sipped her tea. At the end of the working day tea was the drink they all sought. If Ellen had thought about it she could have bought them a cake or offered them biscuits.

Suddenly she became aware of a silence. Not a sweet, kind, satisfied silence as when people pause in their labours, happy with what they have done. This was an active silence, it was working at the job, as if sound was draining into a plug-hole and away. She supposed that the traffic must be running still outside, the birds be singing, this was spring after all, but not a car or a chirp could be heard. The children had stopped playing, Elspeth and Sophy gone quiet.

Yes, there was one bird-call. Then it stopped. As far as she was concerned she had heard the last bird sing.

Then she noticed that other sounds were assembling themselves like a chorus line waiting to come upon the stage. They were small sounds, infant sounds prepared to grow. There was the creaking of wooden timbers. Maggie recognised it for the sound a cart in motion makes, although she had never heard such a sound in intimate connection with her own body before, never been in a cart. Nevertheless, there was a cart, somewhere, and she could hear it. The sound changed and became the noise of wooden wheels rumbling over the cobbles, banging and jolting like a tumbril. Then still wooden, still a wheel, it began to wind itself up, faster, faster like the guillotine beginning its use. The knife would drop.

Metal was clinking on metal, iron on iron. The iron sounded as if it had a cutting edge, and now this metal was scratching across another surface like a knife across a plate.

The scratch, rising to a scream, became near human and fell away into a moan. The moan surely came from a throat.

Although perfectly audible and recognisable, all these were miniature sounds. Tiny but articulate. None of these noises is real, can possibly be real, she told herself, any more than the sound of the sea in a shell held against your ear.

Then, as suddenly as they had come the sounds were gone, and into the void sprang the tick of the kitchen clock, the noise of Sophy laughing, and of Evadne talking to Ellen in a loud voice. Shouting.

Maggie's ears tingled so that she had to shake her head to clear it. She touched one ear, it felt very hot outside and cold as ice inside.

Behind her was a slipslop sound of bare feet. You could tell they were childish feet.

Maggie put down her mug very very carefully, being concerned not to spill a drop, then she turned round to face the walker.

The boy Sam-Tinkerbell stood looking at her, his face calm, his eyes without expression. But it was his throat that caught her horrified gaze. She stared.

Round Sam's throat was a thin shining line of blood as neat and regular as if someone had drawn a line there. She wanted to scream but couldn't, her throat was too stiff and dry.

One of my hallucinations, she thought, one of Maggie's little madnesses. No child, not even Sam, could stand there so calmly gleaming with blood.

Then she saw (how could she not have have noticed it at once, but a cloud of unseeing seemed to have obscured it) that he held in both hands the cheese-cutter, whose wire was bloody red.

With bright eyes, Sam looked at the wire then raised it to his neck again as if to cut into himself again.

Heart pounding, she reached out and took it away, cursing Evadne's carelessness in putting it outside where the child had got at it. Her own carelessness, too. 'Give me that, Sam.' She threw it in the sink. 'Now let me look at your throat.' She was trembling inside, but she kept her voice and hands steady.

He came near, quite docile. Maggie took a clean tissue from her pocket so that she could dab at his cut. Thank goodness it was a shallow slit, not going deep at all, but he bled well, though. The blood was welling up again, even as she dabbed. 'It's not too bad, Sam. You'll need some disinfectant, though. You are a silly boy.' He could have cut his throat right back to the bone with that savage instrument. 'Let's go and see what Mummy can do.' Mummy, she thought with fury, what a help Mummy will be. There she was dreaming in her own lost world while you did that to yourself. 'I expect she's got some bandage to help you with.' I doubt it, she thought, Ellen won't have a thing, she probably expects you to lick yourself better. 'If not,' she went on soothingly, still cleaning him up, 'I've got a First-Aid kit in the car.' She blessed the caution that had made her provide it. Through all this episode she was able to keep her voice light and cheerful, although she felt weak inside as if her guts were falling about loose. Sam was the calm one.

Having staunched the blood more or less, Maggie started to walk Sam towards the garden. They were at the door when Sam pulled away. At the same moment Evadne came in, looking flustered. Sam rushed past.

'What's up with him? Those silly kids have opened—'

Maggie never heard what the children had opened (although she was soon to know), because Ellen was screaming, one high scream after the other. Sounds hurtling into the world with hideous regularity, abusing the ears.

She ran out into the garden. In the paved yard abutting on the kitchen she saw the four of them grouped: Ellen with Sam, screams still rolling out, then Tom and Mary side by side, quite silent.

When Maggie saw what Ellen was doing she felt like screaming herself. Or being sick. A wave of nausea rose up from those loose entrails she was carrying round inside her and hit the back of her throat; she held it back.

Ellen was vainly trying to brush away a black necklace suspended around Sam's throat.

A moving, twisting necklace of black flies that had settled on the wound in the child's throat. As Maggie looked a pendant formed itself, then rose up and flew off in little groups. Not far, they hung around, ready to return. Ellen was pushing them away, but all the time more kept coming.

'Those kids,' said Evadne, 'I told you they opened the meat-safe.'

Sophy, summoned by the screams, had sensibly gone to get the anti-fly spray. Soon she was sending great gusts of it everywhere.

Maggie dragged Sam away from Ellen, and got him into the kitchen by the sink; she sent Elspeth to get her kit from the car, while Evadne dealt with Sam's mother, she didn't care how.

Elspeth slapped Ellen's cheek once very hard, then again. Ellen's screams stopped. During all this time there was never any sound from the children. Not even Sam. Most remarkably not Sam.

By the time Elspeth came back with the disinfectant, Maggie was washing the last fly down the sink and Sophy was spraying the kitchen. Ellen had been resuscitated and was being seated at the kitchen table, in no very tender fashion, by Elspeth.

Maggie patched Sam up, he as passive as ever, and put him in the charge of the other two children who had silently materialised in the kitchen to watch. Mary Powell began to be protective to the child. 'I'll be mother.'

'You be mother then, Mary, but make a better job at it than you did just now.'

Mary blinked, but took the reproof without looking miserable.

'I'll bring you out some fruit juice soon as I can.'

'To the Wendy House?' said Mary-Wendy, surfacing again, after a temporary disappearance.

Maggie nodded. 'To the Wendy House. And keep an eye on Peter and Tinkerbell here.' The Tinkerbell who didn't fly but had flies. Mary was a fragile-boned child with a shining bob of pale hair, out of which her lustrous blue eyes looked full of benign emptiness. It was very hard to pin her down as looking anything, she seemed able to empty herself of any emotion except a calm friendliness. Not conventionally pretty, she had a delicate charm that hooked you. Everyone liked Mary, just as they liked her mother Biddy. What had become of her father? There was a story about him that Maggie could not at that moment remember.

Back in the kitchen she gave Ellen a mug of stewed tea, and advised against any more wine that day.

'You can't take it, Ellen, and that's the truth. Makes you silly. You were silly now.' She let that sink in. 'And you'd better get Sam to the doctor. . . . Tetanus shots and antibiotics and all that.'

Ellen put her head down on her arm and wailed. It was an animal sort of sound that was a measure of Ellen's disintegration. 'It's all that bloody Hallowe'en party. . . . Everything has gone wrong since then; I only did it to get in well with the local peasantry. I had old Mr Christmas to help with the bonfire . . . the kids all love him. I worked myself to a frazzle to give the kids a treat. And what happens? It all went wrong, terribly wrong.'

'So what happened?'

'The fire . . . the fire got out of hand to begin with. . . . But that wasn't it.' She shook her head wearily. 'Oh, it was all shit, all shit.'

Evadne clucked her teeth in disapproval, but Ellen had never learnt not to shock the likes of Evadne. She knew they didn't care for her, even knew why, but couldn't bother to get it right for them. You had to admire her honesty.

'But what happened?' persisted Maggie.

'Sam spoke, you see. Sam recited a whole poem. Kind of a poem. But Sam can't do that sort of thing.' She shook her head again. 'It frightened everyone. No one believed it. I didn't believe it myself. Biddy's gone all frozen and won't speak about it. I don't know.'

'What was the poem?'

'I don't know. It wasn't anything I knew. It sounded like a bit of Shakespeare. . . . Perhaps not a poem.'

Maggie looked at Sam. He looked back at her. There was no poetry in his eyes. If he had ever known a piece of Shakespeare, he did not know it now. Or if he did know it, then he had locked up the knowledge again, and put away the key.

They were late back, a quiet, exhausted carload of cleaners. Maggie dropped them off one by one. Sophy and Elspeth went first, then Evadne, back to baby, mother-in-law (who was looking after the baby) and husband.

'Thank goodness that's all over,' Evadne said gathering up her possessions. She checked them, bag, spectacles and special mop. 'Next cleaning day is Pettit's School? Right?' She moved away. 'Don't want another day like today. Anyway it's over.'

Over for you, Maggie thought, as she drove off, but is it over for me? She didn't think of Sam and Ellen particularly at that point. It had, after all, been real blood on Sam, and for that she was grateful. But her own private little nightmares remained.

As she parked her car she said to herself with conviction: I am an ordinary woman to whom extraordinary things happen.

She remembered the last scrap of her conversation with Ellen that day while the others were getting into the car. She had given Ellen a hug and a kiss for comfort. Ellen had said, 'I don't know what went wrong with my marriage. I tried, really I tried, but it was no good. Somehow it didn't work, not with Nick. . . . How was it with you, Maggie?'

'Oh, it was different with me. . . . I couldn't have children and he minded.' So had she minded, if it came to that.

'I had too many children, I think,' groaned Ellen. 'One too many.'

Sam.

It was a pity she had to break up the conversation then and drive her band home. She might have got more out of Ellen then, if she had stayed, and what happened to Sam might not have happened.

It was no good regarding Sam as an ordinary little boy with an angel shut up inside him, which was how Ellen saw him, or an ordinary little boy with a devil locked up within, which was how some of his peers plainly thought of him, because he was an extraordinary little boy to whom terrible things were happening.

Maggie felt that without wishing to be too explicit about it. Like everyone else in Lukesfield she felt if she didn't think about the situation that was developing, she hoped it would go away.

To her great pleasure David appeared that evening, although they had made no arrangements to meet. He rang her doorbell with his own secret signal, two short rings and one long. In his arms was a bunch of flowers, daffodil and freesia, the ones she loved most. She received the flowers with surprise.

'Did we quarrel?'

'Can't a fellow bring flowers without having had a quarrel?' He gave her a kiss, then a keen look. 'You look whacked. Sit down and have a drink, then I'll take you out to a meal. Nothing grand, mind. Fish and chips most likely, but out.'

'I'd love it. I adore fish and chips. My favourite food.'

'Mine too. . . . Are you ready to go?'

'Just give me a few minutes, will you – I'll go and change.'

Maggie went off in better spirits to shower and put on some fresh clothes. It was one of David's gifts to turn up when needed. If a man did that then you could forgive a lot. She wasn't sure what there was to forgive about David, except for being a policeman, and that might be enough. David's wife had died in childbirth with her child, leaving a pain for him that was so deep and sharp that he was only now able to control it.

It made him very tender with Maggie whose husband had simply walked out and disappeared. Although when she said disappeared she had had one phone call and several bills sent on to her for payment. She just didn't know where he was. David did know where he was, having made it a professional matter to find out. One day he was going to tell Maggie. Maggie, who suspected this, was one day going to ask him just that: Did you come here to investigate my husband? She was going to ask further: What has he done? When this question was answered, the answer would be No; he was investigating someone, but it was not her husband.

As Maggie dressed she knew she was going to give David the story of her day at the right moment that night. He was an easy person to talk to and she did not expect any difficulty. To talk would ease her mind.

Over the meal she did so. Nervously she recounted all her incidents, including but not dwelling upon the last one, the Sam incident. It was already the Sam incident in her own mind, although the blood there was real.

He was the voice of reason, completely matter-of-fact. 'It's probably a form of your migraine, your own variation. You ought perhaps to see your doctor. Otherwise, don't worry. There's nothing to it. That's the rational explanation.'

She agreed. But she was not completely convinced.

'And as for the noises . . . a form of tinnitus. You've had a cold.'

He made it sound so simple. Maggie said, 'Come home and have a glass of wine.' She wanted to get him back into the house, she fancied him tonight. With luck he felt the same. Or she could make him feel the same. They hadn't so far gone to bed together, but it was obviously going to happen soon.

'Love to. I was hoping you'd ask. . . . ' But he hadn't quite dropped the subject of the Wylies. His mind was still moving around it. 'Just as a matter of interest, what was the meat?'

'It was a quarter of venison. Meant to be hung. Why?'

'Just wondering. The thought popped into my mind, and I asked.'

The words were suspended in the air. A quarter of venison. An animal's limbs may be quartered and so may a man's. A man could be hung, drawn and quartered like any beast. It had been done.

Maggie said, 'But what about the boy. What about Sam? What happened there?'

'He wounded himself. He's disturbed. You know yourself that disturbed children can sometimes turn to self-mutilation.

He probably takes in more than his mother believes. He reacts this way. That's how it comes out to me.'

'And the talking? The poem?' She shook her head, wanting to have it all settled.

'I'm not sure if I believe that story as told,' he said thoughtfully. 'I'd like to hear that story from another source.' He didn't believe in poetry really, it was his great deficiency as a man.

She nodded acceptance with a sigh. But what about those flies? That question remained unanswered. 'I expect you're right.'

'But you're not convinced? Come along, love, you know you are in an emotional state. You're overstressed.'

'Are you telling me I am mad?'

'I am not. Would I do that? You're the sanest woman I know. And the nicest. But a vivid imagination you do have.'

He was the detective. It was only a kind of detective story, after all. If you thought of it that way then reason could operate on all details which then became bearable. Tell it is as a detective story, she told herself.

She held up a pleading hand. 'I promise to be a soberer Maggie.' Her hair fell forward on her face, and she pushed it back with a characteristic gesture.

David looked at her with pleasure. There was a sort of feathery disorder to her hair with little tendrils around her neck, and even though he knew this was because she was tired and had been too busy to do her hair properly, it looked elegant and right. How a real woman ought to look. A warm tenderness rose in him. Dear Maggie.

'Come on, let's drive home.' He rose, reaching out a hand and pulling her to her feet. The owner of Larry's Happy Fish Bar watched them go with interest. That was a fine-looking woman. He could fancy her himself. They looked as though they liked each other well enough, and he hoped they were going to do something about it. He had had two wives himself and could easily manage a third.

Inside the house they drank a glass of red wine. Although

Maggie cleaned other people's houses, her own was modestly untidy. It made David like her all the more. It seemed human, somehow, a place to live in. His own house was a tip.

'Mag . . . Can I stay tonight. Please?'

She gave him a brilliant smile, but did not answer.

'I know you're tired. . . . Maybe I shouldn't have asked. But I want to very much.'

'Odd, I do too,' she said softly. 'I'm glad you asked.'

She had looked at the Wylie house as they drove past, not wanting to, but feeling obliged to. Oakwood was in the best part of Lukesfield, abutting on the open area where the gravel pits hid among the scrubland. The school gardens reached it from the other side. Maggie's own house overlooked this patch of ground but did not actually have a boundary with it. There had been one light on in the Wylie house. She didn't like to think of the sort of feelings loose in that lighted room. Sam might love his mother but he couldn't be easy company.

I'm glad I've put clean sheets on the bed, she thought. She was also glad that Kunterhound, her old dog, was dead as he would certainly have clawed David from shoulder to hip if he had found him in bed with Maggie.

She smiled.

'What are you smiling at?'

'Nothing you need to worry about.'

She turned towards him, unbuttoning her dress.

In bed, David said, 'Was it good? Am I allowed to ask?'

'You can always ask.'

'But answer.' He gave her a small slap.

'I'm happy.'

'That's all I wanted to know.'

'Oh, what vanity.'

'Well, it isn't. I care for you, Maggie.'

Silence, satisfied on both sides, both parties thinking things over.

'Why did you make a move tonight? Was it because you were worried about me?'

David continued silent. 'Don't prod. Why spoil something

that was good.'

'But was it?' she insisted. 'Was it?'

'All right. Perhaps there was a bit of that in it. But don't think I didn't want it, because I did. I should think you could tell that.'

'I did. I could. That was the good part. But I felt something else as well.'

'Relax.' He took her in his arms tightly. 'Somehow I want to hang on to you. Stop you flying away.'

'Did you really think I would do that?'

'In a manner of speaking. . . . I felt you might be flying *into* something. Maybe just bad weather.'

'And you're the unimaginative one.'

'I never said that. I just like a practical answer. And there usually is one.'

Like a brain tumour or a little practical treasure like that, thought Maggie.

Next day she went to see her doctor. He listened to her edited but accurate tale of woe. He did not tell her that she had a brain tumour, but reminded her that migraines frequently produced a disturbance in the field of vision, and might produce aural sensations also. He told her that her blood pressure was up, prescribed some treatment, and asked after her hay fever.

'Not bothering me yet,' said Maggie. 'I'm hoping not to have it this year.' She did not reveal to him that she had consulted a hypnotist.

Her doctor, for his part, did not reveal how attracted to her he was, never more so than now, which was the reason he was so professional with her.

Next week there was a school holiday at Miss Pettit's academy and the High-Lo team moved in for a full day's cleaning. This was the second time they had done so. It was hard work but usually they enjoyed it because Biddy made them so welcome and the school nurse always saw they had a delicious meal. The meal was as good as ever, but somehow none of them had much appetite.

Two weeks later Sam was reported missing.

Reported missing, but some people said that he had been gone for some time before Ellen reported his absence.

During the time Sam was missing there were several small fires at Pettit's School which were blamed on the children, but which might have been spontaneous. One in a waste-basket, another in the garden. Just small fires, but alarming.

Chapter Two

What Ellen had reported to the police was lacking in detail, and strangely told. Strangely, because she was calm and quiet, and had so little to tell.

She appeared in the Lukesfield police station in the early evening of April 30th, a Wednesday, and reported that her younger son, Sam, aged eight years and a few months, and 'difficult', had disappeared from his home that morning.

This is what she said happened: she had gone shopping, leaving Sam at home. 'What, alone?' she was asked. She had nodded assent. 'Yes, alone.' There was a pause before she added: 'Locked in. In his room.'

This produced a mild sensation in the police station, it not being what mothers in Lukesfield (or policemen either) considered the correct way to behave, especially with difficult children. But locked in or not, Sam had got out of his room and gone. His bedroom door was open and the door to the garden had been opened and left open. This door had been locked also, but the key left in it. The key had been left in his bedroom door.

Could Sam unlock the door? Either door? Yes, in theory, but he had never done so. Did he have another key?

Ellen made a bad impression on the police who took her statement. She seemed to be leaving out more than she put in. It was the young constable who took the notes of the conversation who started the rumour that Sam had been gone longer than Ellen admitted. She didn't sound right, he said, from the depths of his vast experience, she was covering up. What he said to himself, although nothing would have got him to admit this to his colleagues, was that she sounded like a woman who had lost her heart.

Ellen answered the questions they put to her, but there was a sort of looseness and vagueness to her replies that puzzled them. Yes, she could name the shops, yes, she could rough out the time she had been in them, but she let them feel that she doubted if anyone would remember her.

'When I came back I ran round looking for Sam. I was frantic. I can't really remember what I did.' She wasn't crying, but she was close to it. 'Now I've come to you. Please find Sam for me.'

After she had seen the police Ellen knew she had to tell Nicholas. When she had done so, she put the telephone down on his angry roar and went outside to be sick. In his angry moods Nicholas frightened her. She granted he was right to be angry now, but she knew nothing could stop her stomach reacting. He had been known to hit her.

Nicholas told Biddy who was shocked and appalled, and (this she would never have admitted to Nicholas) terrified. She caught the breath of disaster. She was passionately in love with Nicholas, she longed for them to be married, but Ellen and Sam combined, like some monster figure, a Samellen or an Ellensam, she could not separate them in her mind, seemed to stand for ever between her and Nicholas.

So Biddy heard the news with foreboding, passing on the news to her daughter Mary with careful editing. Sam had gone away she said, he'd be back but Mary must not expect to find him at home for a few days. At this cautious phrasing Mary looked justifiably puzzled. But she was too wise to ask questions. She did not want her mother to marry Nicholas who did not look like good stepfather material to her, but she had sense enough not to let her mother see this too clearly. Thus she had pretended to be just a little bit fonder of Sam and Tom than she really was. She did like them, but felt she could live without them if she had to and really might prefer to. She was a quiet imaginative child, mature beyond her years. Biddy worried about her.

Maggie heard the news from Ellen. She had had a hard working day which she was glad to have done with when suddenly there was Ellen, sitting on her doorstep, waiting.

Maggie was fumbling for her door key, having garaged her

car, when she became aware of this figure hunched on the step in the dark. She gave a little scream of alarm.

'Oh Maggie, it's only Ellen. Oh, I'm so glad to see you. Something's happened so terrible that I can hardly bear to tell you.'

She was going to, though, Maggie could see that. It was absolutely clear, Ellen was going to tell her all, and she was not particularly pleased to see the girl. Tired and grubby after a day of cleaning the local antique shop, what Maggie wanted was a drink and a bath. 'What is it?'

'You're my only friend here, Maggie, so I had to come.'

'Am I?' Maggie was reluctant to be Ellen's only friend, it could turn out to be a full-time occupation. She didn't think she had the energy left from her own life to put into it. 'What is it? What's up?'

'Sam, it's Sam, I've lost him. He's gone.'

'Gone where?' A stupid question, Maggie realised at once. She put an arm round Ellen's shoulders and led her into the house. 'Come on in and tell me about it. . . . Wait a minute, before we do anything else, have you let the police know?'

'Oh yes, yes. That's what's upsetting me. Well, partly. As well as Sam, that is.' Ellen was incoherent, but quite sober. 'They think it's me, somehow, that I've done him harm. They don't say so, but I feel it.'

She took Ellen into the kitchen, switched on the kettle and then accidentally but on purpose broke a cup. Perhaps that would do for her share of bad luck.

Ellen heard the noise but took no notice. Broken crockery was a commonplace in her life.

'Come on, Ellen. Get it out. Sam's gone. I've got that. But how did it happen? What did happen? Explain a bit more.'

She did not have much hope that Ellen would explain, explaining was something Ellen was not very good at, but it seemed necessary to get her talking.

'I left Sam on his own while I went shopping. . . . Biddy Powell had taken the school on an expedition to the British Museum. Sam doesn't go on expeditions like that. Naturally. . . . Anyway, he hasn't been at school much lately. . . . I thought, he'll be all right. . . . I shut him in the house.' She shook her head. 'But when I got home he was gone.'

Maggie made the tea, carefully warming the pot, then adding the tea-bags and letting it infuse. Everyone said that with modern tea-blends nothing of this mattered, but she thought it did. Besides, she was considering Ellen's statement. 'Gone' didn't seem much of an explanation.

'How long were you out?'

'A couple of hours. Perhaps longer.'

'And Sam was shut up in the house on his own? Locked in?'

It made an appalling picture: the boy imprisoned on his own and then left for hours. No wonder the police hadn't liked it, no one could do.

Maggie said gently, 'That was a very silly thing to do, Ellen.'

'I had so many errands,' began Ellen, and then, as Maggie looked sceptical: 'You don't know what it was like being shut up for hours and hours on my own with Sam. . . . It was bad enough when I had Nick, but on my own . . . I had to have some relief.'

It was no good nagging at the moment; Ellen needed comfort, not upbraiding. 'He hasn't been gone for very long. It's only been a little while. He'll come back.' If he knew his way around – he was usually shepherded everywhere. But no one could be sure exactly what Sam knew or didn't know. It was a secret he kept locked up inside him. There was no doubt that Sam was an unpredictable bundle. What he knew and what he chose to do could not be counted upon. 'Or if he doesn't come back, then he'll be found. It hasn't been long. Give the police a chance.'

After a pause Ellen said: 'It *has* been long.'

'How long?' Maggie put the question quickly.

After another pause, Ellen said, 'It could have been all this morning . . . and then into the afternoon a bit. I was away rather a long time. . . . I left him things to eat in his room. Then I was looking for Sam. I roamed around for ages. The hours seemed to melt away. I didn't tell the police exactly how long because I'm not sure. I was frightened. I'm telling you.'

And I wish you weren't, thought Maggie. But she realised that Ellen was irresistibly drawn towards her as a confessor figure. Somehow, fate had allotted her this part.

'I was out looking for him . . . all the time.'

How she did harp on the passage of time. Maggie poured out the tea, gave Ellen a cup, and took her own up. 'Drink it and let me think.'

'Thank you, Maggie.' Ellen accepted the implied offer of support. The tea was good and hot, she began to relax a little.

'I want to get one thing clear. Was Sam capable of getting out of the house on his own? Unlocking the door and so on? I mean could he have done it? Did you lock him into his room or just in the house?' *Just*, she said to herself, condemning her on the use of the word, because even that made a rotten enough picture. Ellen had asked for trouble and she had got it.

'I thought I'd locked him in his room, but I might have forgotten.' Ellen dropped her eyes, fully conscious of the admission she had made.

'This isn't the first time you've left Sam locked in the house, is it? How often have you done it, Ellen?'

Ellen put her lips together and wouldn't answer. Finally she muttered something about once or twice.

'You weren't out shopping, were you? Tell the truth. You were meeting someone. A man?' Who else? Nothing ambivalent about Ellen. Only one sex she fancied. 'The one who telephoned you? The one who calls you Bunty?'

'No, not him. He's out. He's dirt. Yes, I was with someone, but someone who respects me. I was with him. But I told the police I was shopping. I should think you could understand that.'

'Did they believe you?' Doubtful, thought Maggie, since I didn't.

'I don't know. They weren't very nice to me. Hostile, the pigs, almost rude.'

'Did you call them pigs then?'

'No, of course not. I was as nice as I know how. Lot of good that does round here.' Ellen's big blue eyes glowed with anger. She had never looked more engaging. She was a beautiful creature even now with her hair uncombed, her lips pale and chewed. Probably what maddened the women of Lukesfield was the way Ellen neglected such natural advantages. What maddened the men was only too clear. And that didn't improve her standing with local matrons either. Maggie sighed. She felt jealous herself.

The two women sat in silence for a few minutes. Maggie poured out another cup of tea.

Then Maggie thought of something. 'So where's Tom?' She had forgotten about Tom. No doubt he was used to it, poor little chap. He had the look of a boy who was constantly overlooked.

Tom was with his father. Nicholas had swept in and taken him away. Ellen thought he would be staying with her mother-in-law.

'She hates me,' said Ellen. 'I can see why, but I don't hate her. That's funny, isn't it? She's a nice woman.' She sounded perplexed, but accepting.

Ellen and her Sam had more in common than might have been suspected. They both found the world a puzzle and the human race hard to read.

Silently considering this, Maggie went to her refrigerator. 'You'd better have a meal. When did you last eat? I'm hungry myself. Cheese omelette do?'

'Yes, please. . . . Can I stay the night?'

'No.' Maggie had no hesitation, the reply came out with speed. She knew where she stood on that one. There *was* a limit; she would soothe Ellen, reason with her, even comfort her, but have her stay in the house she would not.

Ellen accepted the rebuff silently, like a little cat that was used to being pushed away. It said something about her relationship with Nicholas. Still, she must have done some pushing away herself. That always had to be remembered.

'I love Sam,' she said suddenly. 'Don't believe anything else whatever people say. I just need out occasionally. And I have needs and wants like anyone else. I may not have been the world's best wife, but I was faithful to Nicholas till he left. It was he that left *me*, don't forget. I didn't leave him. And I love him too, for your information. Still love him,' she added, half to herself.

The omelette, one large rich cheese omelette divided between the two of them, was good. Maggie felt better after the meal, while she saw that Ellen seemed calmer. Since she looked like settling down for a long session, Maggie said, 'Must do the dishes.' She stood up.

'You want to get rid of me.'

'You'll be better off at home. That's where Sam will come back to.'

'Think so? I hate that house. And the garden. It gets on my nerves. I tried sitting out there to get out of the house but it was no good. The garden is the worst. It makes me miserable. How do you feel about your garden?'

'Nothing special. I never think about it.'

Ellen slowly and reluctantly made her way to the front door, still talking. 'What can I do about Sam, I feel so helpless.'

'You can only wait. Leave it to the professionals, to the police.' This was the voice of David talking through Maggie. The police answer to a problem.

'They don't know Sam like I do.'

But who did know Sam, Maggie asked herself? Perhaps his contemporaries at school knew him as well as anyone, treating him, as far as she could see, with a mixture of awe and friendliness.

'Have you asked the children what they know?'

'Biddy spoke to them. No use. They didn't know anything.'

The relationship between Ellen and Biddy was a complicated one, but apparently they kept open a channel of communication.

'It might be a good idea to listen to them. Not to what they say to you but what they say to each other.'

She could do that herself. Her team were going to clean the windows at Pettit's the next week. She knew from experience you heard a lot on a task like that one.

Ellen continued her absent-minded progress to the door, still thinking aloud. If Ellen's processes could be called thought – they sometimes seemed more like spontaneous combustion.

'Tom might say something to me. If I ever see him again, which I won't if Nick can manage it. . . . But Tom doesn't talk to me these days. I don't know what's gone wrong. . . . I let him and Mary play together, she's such a nice child. Tom isn't nice, too like his father, but he's bright. It hasn't worked out, though.' Nothing did work out for Ellen, not even her looks, or her genuine, if small, acting talent, there seemed a jinx on her. It was what old-fashioned people called 'character', no doubt. But character is a combination of inheritance, environment and luck. You had to count in the luck.

The telephone rang, but Maggie ignored it. She guessed it was David, but he could ring again. It was as well to keep him in suspense.

Ellen did not seem to hear the telephone which showed how far she was in another world. 'I'm off. I expect you're glad to get rid of me. I know I'm a liability, but thanks, Maggie. You don't know how grateful I am.'

'I'll walk home with you.'

'No, I'm all right. What can happen to me that's worse than what has?' She put her hand to her pocket. 'Yes, I've got the house keys. Wouldn't do to have to ask the police to let me in, would it?' She gave a small, bleak smile.

A yellow, plastic tube-shaped object fell out of her pocket and to the ground. With an exclamation she bent down to pick it up. 'That's Sam's. His favourite toy. His yellow submarine. I've been carrying it around for luck. . . . I mean luck for Sam.'

'Ellen, your hand. . . . You've hurt yourself. Come back into the kitchen where I can look.' Maggie pulled the girl back towards the well-lighted kitchen. 'There's blood on your hand.' She touched the stain.

Ellen looked at her hand in surprise. 'No. No, I haven't. I'm all right. There's nothing there.'

Maggie blinked.

'Nothing there,' repeated a bewildered Ellen.

'My mistake,' she told Ellen. 'Just an optical illusion. I get them sometimes before an attack of migraine.' But inside she was frightened at this extension of her delusion to the sense of touch. It seemed so unlikely and ominous, somehow.

Ellen went quiet and protested no more, but she seemed concerned. Together they went through to the garden and out to the road. Behind them the front door was left wide open with all the lights blazing against the night. The air was warm and sweet, a tranquil spring evening in a pleasant place to live. Lukesfield was pleasant, Maggie always told herself, adding that she was lucky to live there, as all the house-agents' advertisements confirmed, saying how good it was for children with so much open space in which to play and so much fresh air.

The houses all around were filled by prosperous, productive families with more than the usual complement of motor-cars, video recorders, word-processors and children. Next door to Maggie lived Billy and Fabia: Billy was in insurance and Fabia in advertising, so far childless in this marriage, although both had offspring from earlier alliances. Beyond them was a well-known writer and his lovely young wife: the third edition – he always went into lots of editions, Lukesfield said they were getting cheaper and larger. The other side of Maggie was a tiny little house (by the standards of Lukesfield, only one bathroom) occupied by the widow of a diamond merchant. At Christmas and all public holidays she glittered brighter than any Christmas tree, even at other times there was a constant flicker from hands and ears as from some small, luminous marine creature. All these houses and others beyond were lit up, and in all of them were the enemies of Ellen, talking about her.

It might not be like that in fact, reflected Maggie, but after prolonged contact with Ellen a little persecution phobia seemed to rub off.

'Look after your headache, Maggie. You've been good to me. I need someone.'

'Do my best.' Maggie tried to sound jocund.

Something terrible was happening to them both, but they must hang on to the feeling that underneath all was well, all would be well. There was more than a chance of grace somewhere.

A vision of something horrible flashed across her eyes, quick as a blink.

Maggie went back into her own house, without any more conversation; she did not want to talk to Ellen about her migraine and its symptoms. She would never again mention what she had seen. Or what she seemed to have seen. The preliminary to a migraine it might be, but it felt like a preview of hell.

Years ago, when she was in love with her husband, but not yet married to him, they had visited a fifteenth-century church in a small Cotswold town. One great window had shown Christ in Glory with, beneath his feet, the Day of Judgement and the Harrowing of Hell. The damned looked up, showing their pale and frantic faces, their limbs angular, livid and distorted.

Maggie's companion had murmured something sophisticated about comparing it with Bosch, but for Maggie the window was infinitely more terrifying than any picture by Bosch. Bosch knew what he was doing, in a way he was playing a game with his audience, enjoying his own scenes of torment, a bit of a sadist. But the maker of the window had believed in the utter reality of what he had shown, it was a simple statement of faith, no joke about it.

Then she had seen writhing bodies, rising from the grave, and this picture came back to torment her. In memory she saw a torso, a woman's body, stretched out with limbs extended. There were no hands, just stumps cut at the wrists. No legs, no head, simply a severed neck.

This vision was in grisaille, but none the more bearable for that. This terrible sight had flashed upon her eyes, then disappeared at subliminal speed. Here, then gone.

Perhaps she had imagined it all? If not, as an extension of her migraine she could do without it. Tinnitus was to be preferred. It had been a silent vision.

She took a tablet to ward off the migraine as instructed by her doctor, and then placed herself in a chair to do her deep, slow breathing exercises as prescribed by her hypnotist. At such a time she was instructed to set her mind on something soothing. So she settled on David, which perhaps was a compliment he might not have appreciated. Does any man like to feel he is soothing?

She closed her eyes, feeling better already and wondering if she could drift to sleep. She did not expect to dream of a bloody body, for whatever she had seen or heard, it had always been a daylight horror not a nightmare.

She sat for little while trying to meditate on a desert island with David, a warm beach, the sun on her face. . . . No good, thoughts would obtrude. It came to her that the head, arms and legs of the body had not been severed, that they were still *there* (wherever there was) but were extended, tied down, outside her field of vision.

Whether this made the picture more bearable or worse she could not say at the moment. On the whole she thought it was worse, since this circus of arms and legs was stretched out for a purpose.

She opened her eyes, while still breathing deeply, and tried to be reasonable. She knew that migraines did you no harm in the long run. Whatever the visual disturbance produced by the dilation or contraction of the tiny blood vessels (there it was, blood again), you were none the worse for it afterwards. She must not imagine more than was happening.

What the eye did not see was not there: what the eye saw was not there, either. Cling to that thought, Maggie.

Slowly, and still carrying on with the careful breathing, she began to prepare for bed. Skin and hair received attention. Her face in the looking glass shining with cream was pale and thoughtful, but healthy enough. She rejected the idea of a serious illness. She was not incubating a brain tumour: she would have none of that.

She continued to reason with herself. The fact, noticed today, that the migraine attacks were precipitated by the mention of, or the presence of, Sam could be understood, because she was anxious about the boy. He worried her, thus he produced stress, and the stress produced the migraine. Simple. Just don't think too much about Sam.

Carefully, gently she breathed in and out, filtering out all thoughts of Sam. Her mind went quiet and dead. Somewhere, at the back of it, a dark thought, like a little rodent, was gnawing away at her peace.

So she telephoned David. Her message was very short. Please come over and stay. Tonight I do not wish to be alone.

'Coming over.' He sounded pleased to be asked.

Within the hour he was there, bearing a cauliflower and

daffodils from his garden. This was how he brought a woman gifts. 'For you to eat and for you to look at. . . . Give the daffs a good drink, and use the cauliflower this week, while it's fresh. Don't leave it around to get stale like the last one. You do eat I suppose, when I'm not here?' He was bubbling over with enjoyment of life. 'By the way, my house will need your outfit again soon. It's going downhill fast.'

It was how they had met. Maggie's team had been hired to clean his bungalow. Like all the houses they were hired to work in, it was neglected. Almost tidy, almost clean, was how she put it to herself. David had tried, but not hard enough. She had never discovered how he had found out about her and High-Lo, but he had rung up one day and placed the order. Then he had returned in time to pay the bill. They had gone on from there.

Now he was the voice of reason, as always.

'Look, you've been working hard, knocking yourself to bits making a success of High-Lo. Stands to reason it's going to show up. Just take the tablets the doctor gave you and relax.'

'I expect you're right.'

'I know I am. . . . Have a brain scan if you're worried.'

Maggie wondered briefly what electronic wonders would do to the pictures in her mind. Whether it would wipe them out or blow them up into something much worse? Either seemed possible.

David was still being soothing.

'And then there's the business of the boy Sam being missing. Naturally you don't like that. It's nasty.'

He knew all about the boy being missing, had been expecting questions from her. More questions than had come.

'What do you have on it? Do you know something I don't know?'

'I only know what you do: that he's missing.' His voice was grave. Although a policeman, he was not a detective, he had always been in the uniformed branch, and was now mostly involved in adminstration of one sort or another. He was rising higher and higher and could expect one day, perhaps, to be a Chief Constable, or possibly proceed to some high rank in the Metropolitan Police. He was hopeful.

He was hopeful too about Maggie. Many things had gone wrong in his life, but not that one. Still he had to be careful with her, not push her too hard. 'I know he's missing. But I know also there's a bad feeling around that his mother is not telling all the truth. You know her. Could that be so, do you think?'

Reluctantly Maggie nodded. She didn't want to give Ellen away, but the boy had his rights too. 'Truth and Ellen are soon parted.'

'Keep away from her, that's my advice.' It was advice soberly given and soberly received, although Maggie knew she could not abandon Ellen lightly. A kind of promise of mutual support had passed between them, hadn't it? 'Don't let her get too close.'

Easier said than done; Ellen was close already. 'I'll try.' She felt more comfortable in her mind with David there.

All the same, she was glad that Ellen had taken away Sam's toy when she went. Toys are closely associated with their owner and she found Sam alarming. She was surprised that Sam had left his plaything behind when he went, but perhaps he had no choice. She knew she did not want it in the house, and thank goodness Ellen had taken it.

But when Maggie went into the kitchen to make the two of them a nightcap she found that Ellen had not.

There was the yellow submarine winking away on the kitchen table like a light. Quickly Maggie picked it up and tucked it away in a drawer.

Tomorrow she would see her doctor again and say is it possible to see phantoms with migraine? And he would say No and suggest some more tablets. Another dose, another cure. Then she would go to see her hypnotist and would ask the same question and he would have no answer.

Nevertheless, in spite of her worries, Maggie was asleep, satisfied and content, before David. He stayed awake long enough to hear her quiet breathing.

He was coming to love her very much. He loved her warmth, her delicacy of spirit, her occasional boisterousness; he knew he wanted to keep her safe. It would be better if she did not see too much of Ellen Wylie. All his experience as a policeman was warning him away from Ellen. Every story he heard about her made him suspicious. In some way that he could not quite make out she was a liar. He feared her intrusion into Maggie's life.

As for the boy Sam he could see no happy outcome there. The boy must be dead. And being dead, you had to ask some questions.

Who could want the boy out of the way? Who could find the means to spirit him out of his own house? Who was close enough to Sam, who had enough emotion involved to want to do him harm?

The answer came back pretty quick: only a member of his family. And of that family the most likely person was Ellen.

Ellen seemed the obvious candidate. The fact that Maggie reported her as thoroughly distressed and wretched meant nothing. She *would* be unhappy. In despair, probably, but, in his book, guilty all the same.

He resolved to speak to his friends in the CID to find out all they knew. There was something very unpleasant going on in Lukesfield and he needed to know more.

Ellen had no migraine to worry about, saw no blood, conjured up no bloody phantoms, but had plenty of ghosts in her house all the same, all making themselves at home and acting out their histories.

Sam was everywhere and all the time, of course, but at the moment it was Nicholas she was seeing.

He was there in the big living room, alone with her as he had been on that day on which they had first moved into the house. He had chosen the wallpaper, the curtains and the carpet, taking her for a special trip to David Hicks's shop in Jermyn Street to show her what he wanted, and then managing to find materials very similar (only not quite so good, Ellen had thought) elsewhere at less expense. It was typical of Nicholas's plundering ways. One of the things, apart from Sam, that had drawn them apart; Ellen did not plunder.

Ellen's mother had told Ellen to stand up for herself. 'You were a good actress once. Act firm with him even if you don't feel it. You let that man walk all over you.'

Ellen had bowed her head in assent to her mother, but not

done much about it. Let her try, she had thought to herself. Let her try standing up to Nicholas. He could be like a juggernaut on the move, when he chose.

Biddy Powell seemed able to halt the idol on his cart without throwing herself underneath it. No one had ever suggested that Nicholas walked over her. It's my own fault, Ellen told herself, I bring out the worst in everyone.

There Nicholas was now, explaining to her how beautifully the dark blue brocade of the curtains set off the wallpaper which was green with touches of silver, and how there must always be lots of flowers (fresh flowers, Ellen, not dead or dying like you usually do) and how she must try to 'bring the garden into the house'.

Ellen hated the idea of the garden creeping into the house but she did her best with branches of flowering blossoms and leaves from the trees. The garden had got in all right, and now there would be no getting it out.

Some time later Sam was born. He was a beautiful child with the good looks of both his parents apparent even in infancy to a remarkable degree. When it became clear that there was something subtly wrong with Sam, that he did not respond as other children did to the world around him, Ellen knew whose fault it was. Hers. The doctors and Nicholas urged her to accept it as a kind of accident of life for which no one was to blame, but Ellen knew better.

She accepted the burden of her guilt, and took Sam on her shoulders to love and to carry for the rest of her life.

Naturally, bearing this burden she had to put others down, and Nicholas and Tom were deposited to stand on their own two feet without help from her, even though they asked her not to drop them, especially Tom who was only a little boy and did not like being dumped. (It took Nicholas some time to notice that *he* had been dumped, and he minded then all right.)

Tom was the ghost in the nursery where he had spent many hours alone with Patrizia, their Italian au pair. Ellen never wondered what had become of Patrizia, she knew without being told: she had married her German boy friend and lived in Munich. It was her fate.

Tom's little ghost mouthed a few lonely words at her before turning into the active, aggressive little boy who went to Miss Pettit's School and knew how to swear. Picked that up from me, Ellen deplored, but Biddy Powell, his soon-to-be loving stepmother, would know how to deal with it.

Ellen tried to ignore the ghosts of her elder son and her husband that night to concentrate on Sam's. He was all over the house! On the stairs, in the kitchen, in the bathroom and in the great living room which was still grubby. All of High-Lo's efforts had not got out the dirt which Ellen has so carefully ground in. The room Nicholas loved most must be the room she destroyed first, although she hadn't done a bad job on the rest of the house.

In Sam's room, personal and private to him, she did a thing she almost never did. She started to tidy up. The police had asked to look over Sam's room, taking the opportunity to give the whole house a good scrutiny, and she could still remember the way they had looked at the mess. Beasts.

She could smell the police in the room.

Methodically she moved around, putting away clothes, shoes and toys. Sam had taken nothing with him. Nothing. Not his favoured toy, nor his woolly blanket that he sucked as he slept, nor his toothbrush which he adored and rarely used unless told.

The toothbrush had been made of china specially for Sam with his name painted on it. He really loved that brush. He had a mug to match with his intials on it. Tom had one as well, which had certainly gone with him.

But something Sam had taken with him. He had taken her purse with all her money in it. Her household keys were in the purse too, but she had a spare set. Of this loss Ellen had said nothing. Especially, she had not told the police.

She could not admit to the loss of the purse because she would have had to explain why she had not needed the money to go shopping. And why she had not needed her keys to get back into the house.

A question better not asked.

It took time to make Sam's room appear orderly, but it was done in the end. Now his room looked bare, without character.

Sam was truly gone from it. Unconsciously Ellen had made it look as if she did not expect him back. This had been very far from her intention but it was what she had done.

Then she went to her own bedroom, the large room she had shared with Nicholas. She looked at the tumbled, disordered bed where a person had not been happy, where a person had struggled hard to get some happiness out of the only activity of love left to her and had found it not there for the asking.

The ghost in that room was her own.

Once again, though, she saw a hard piece of concrete evidence that the police had overlooked because its significance was lost upon them.

A clock, a small cheap alarm clock of the type sold in a chain of chemists. Not at all the sort of clock the room was designed for, nor the clock that Nicholas would have bought, but just the sort of clock that someone hard-up and not caring about style, simply wanting an alarm to ring to remind them of the time would buy. That sort of clock. The alarm was set to ring at five o'clock.

Ellen picked up the clock and tucked it away in a drawer, much as Maggie had secreted the yellow submarine.

She felt tired and depressed; with the idea that it might improve her spirits she moved towards the shower room in one corner of the bedroom, peeling off her clothes and letting them drop behind her as she went.

The bedroom was large and as carefullly designed by Nicholas as the rest of the house; he had created a long, narrow room with a balcony overlooking the garden, with the bed raised on a dais in the centre. It was a melodramatic room, which was one side of Nicholas he kept private.

She shut herself in the shower-closet, turned on the water, and leaned back, letting the extremely hot water bounce off her body. She liked the look of her body better when it was wet these days, now that she was so much heavier. She had put on weight since Nicholas had left her, letting her waist and thighs fill up with a deposit of flesh that had never been there before. Some people thought that it improved her face and breasts: Ellen thought it ruined her.

She hated the girl inside that body that lived in that house.

Relaxing under the rush of water, she did not hear that someone had entered the house.

Nicholas let himself in as noisily as he could. God knows he was angry enough with Ellen, but he did not want to frighten her to death. He could imagine the state she must be in, and some residual tenderness towards her remained.

He had thought of ringing the doorbell, but it was still his house, if no longer his home, and he had a lawyer's sense of possession. The same attitude applied to Ellen; she was still his wife with certain rights and duties.

He banged the door behind him, giving her due warning, and shouted her name. 'Ellen? Ellen, are you here?'

He advanced into the hall where he saw her coat thrown across the stairs. 'I know you are, damn you.'

He had called her Angel Face when they first moved into the house. Ellen was a girl to summon up pet names, love names, like Bunty, but hate names also.

'Ellen? It's Nick. Come on out, I want you.' He was going rapidly from room to room, turning on lights, calling her name, getting more and more angry. 'Ellen? You upstairs? I'm coming up.'

At the top of the stairs, he paused; he could hear the shower. Then it stopped. 'Ellen, I know you're in there. Come out.'

He banged on the door; she could hear him all right. 'Get out of there, I want to talk to you.'

Behind the door Ellen cowered against the wall of the shower, listening.

'Out, Ellen, out.' He was banging on the door so that it shook.

'I'm never going to open that door,' Ellen told herself. 'Never. In a little while he will go away.' She never learnt about Nicholas; he did not go away.

Her husband put his shoulder to the door and pushed it open. Ellen was crouched against the opposite wall with a towelling robe held tightly around her. She stared at him silently. 'Get up.' He pulled her to her feet. 'I want to talk to you. Tom's been telling me things. He says you beat Sam. Is that what you do? Is that what you've done now? Where is he? Come on, Ellen.' He was shaking her. 'I want to know.'

'No, no.' The words were jerked out of her. 'I never beat Sam.' She was never going to admit she beat Sam. 'It's not like that. Tom is lying.'

'He is not lying. I know when my son is telling the truth. And I know when you're lying, too. I ought to beat you myself. Where is he? What have you done to him?'

'Nothing, nothing.' She was screaming.

'You *will* tell me.' He shook her.

'Look at my arms, look at them. Bruises there. Sometimes I beat myself. There is guilt around, so someone has to be beaten, because there has to be punishment, but not Sam.'

It was as near to the truth as he was going to get. Suddenly sickened by his own violence, Nicholas released her. He felt exhausted, with all emotion and energy drained away. 'God, what a mess this place is. . . . I'm going, Ellen. If you have anything to tell me about Sam, tell me now.' He waited, but she said nothing.

So he left her there in the bedroom, no longer crying, but just siting on the bed looking at her bare arms. He ran down the stairs and out of the house. The scent of the polishes and bleaches which the High-Lo team had used still hung about the place, but above it the house was producing its own smell of desolation, the rising damp of misery.

Sam looked up to see a green, blue and white pattern above him that reminded him of the wallpaper in the big room at home. He did not put that thought into words, but he experienced it. He was living proof that, contrary to some philosophical opinion, you do not have to use words to form precise thoughts. (Words for Sam were more enemies than informers, speaking with an alien tongue.) At this moment his thought was that what he saw was familiar and homelike.

Comforting. In his life he had needed comforting, not always received it from those who should have given it to him. Nor could he always have accepted it if offered. For him life was lived as behind a barrier of glass, through which he could see but which made communication difficult. His glass bell covered him from head to foot, so completely shielding and obstructing him that sometimes when Ellen reached out for him he could not be sure if she had touched him or he had touched her. Or whether the touch had been violent or soft. Did he feel pain or was Ellen feeling it? He genuinely did not know. But he knew enough to sense the question rumbling away inside him, unanswered, but exploding, on occasion, into a situation that might be Sam hitting Ellen or Ellen hitting Sam, the two being interchangeable.

Where Sam was *now* was his new home. He had been told so by someone he trusted. This had not been put into words, but by the manner of his installation he knew it was so. He felt as much at home as he ever did, which was not much; he was contented enough. No more strange than at Oakwood.

Idly he picked at the scab around his throat where he had carved a channel with the cheese wire. On that occasion it had been his neck that he cut, but on another occasion it might be some other animal's. A little blood stained his finger; he licked it, enjoying the taste. It reminded him of the tall, soft-bosomed lady who had put a bandage round his throat, he thought of her with real liking. If he had been in the habit of using such words he would have called her Maggie, my darling. He knew the emotion if not the word. There was a group who were his darlings; Ellen was one, Mary Powell another, so was Tom. Nicholas was not.

Now he stretched out a hand to other alien limbs and began to pick at them, too. Little bits flew about without pain. Suddenly warming to his task he began to transfer fragments of his new home from one place to another, showing in his job a pleasure in the ceaseless repetition.

It was a comfort to do such work. At no point did he think: I am lost, I will be sought for, I ought to go home, because as far as he was concerned he had never been found.

During the next week David spoke to his police mates about the missing boy. His longest conversation was with his closest friend in the CID for the area, Chief Superintendent Toller. Ted

Toller passed very little information back because there was little to tell. As he said, child disappearances were always a bugger.

The story as the police believed they had established it was simple. Ellen had gone out leaving her son shut up alone in the house; he was locked into his room. When she got back after shopping he had gone and the door to the garden was swinging open. On being pressed she said she could not be sure she had locked this door or, for that matter, any of the others. She thought she had or she would not have left Sam behind but she might have been careless. Then in a panic she had run around looking for Sam. Finally – too late, in their opinion – she had gone to the police.

'No sign of a struggle or a break-in. So if an outsider got in and took the boy the house was either unlocked or he had a key,' said the Chief Superintendent. 'Or, the boy let himself out. No evidence he could not use a key if he had one. No evidence that he *could*, either, or that he had keys. No evidence, in short. As for the mother, we don't trust her tale but can't fault it. Nor can she prove it. She named the stores where she stopped, but no one remembers her. Nothing remarkable in that – big shops and a busy day.'

The police search had been thorough and intensive, but no sign of Sam had been found. Thus the Chief Superintendent's tale. But during the whole case he was struck by David's anxiety about Maggie, which, for some reason he could not be sure of, perturbed him. The whole affair stayed in his mind so that he spoke of it as he played golf with Arthur Chamberlain, his dentist and neighbour. Arthur Chamberlain, in his turn, mentioned it over bridge that evening to his friend, Henry Shaw, the editor of the local paper. Arthur's wife, who was dealing the next hand, said: 'You always were a scientist manqué, Arthur, stop trying to be a detective as well, and get on with the game.'

In the same period Maggie saw her doctor and was given a letter to take to the hospital, and saw her hypnotist.

All the circles were now in touch.

Chapter Three

The police were searching for Sam in their usual thorough, routine way. A picture of him looking angelic had appeared on the television screens of the local network. No come-back.

Everywhere, every place available and unavailable, where he could have hidden was searched. More than once in some cases just to be sure. All disused refrigerators, motor-cars, and rubbish bins on the Lukesfield rubbish tip were opened and checked. Again, no come-back.

The searchers were young but experienced men, who had been trained to search the ground. They kept their heads down as they searched, prodding the earth with poles. At intervals heads were raised and swung up and around so that all horizons were covered. It was professionally done, they took in all they were meant to take in: each disturbance of the ground, each piece of litter, every scrap of paper received its due attention. They were fully adult men with childhood long left behind: what they did not see did not exist, and what they saw with adult gaze was what adults usually see, exactly what was there and no more.

In a hollow in the ground a pool had formed with water drawn from an underground stream which surfaced the other side of Lukesfield. In the middle of the pool was a small island covered with low bushes and slender, stunted trees. The vegetation was so thick in patches that little tunnels could be made in it. There were many footprints around the water's edge as if people came and went across a miniature causeway of broken stones.

The police searched carefully, but found nothing.

'Not saying he hasn't been there, but he's not there now. No one is. Old tramp's hide-away, I'd say,' said one young man, mopping his brow.

As far as the police knew, an angel could have come down from heaven and picked Sam up. Or an alien in a spaceship from another world if you were into another kind of fantasy.

Or, as they suspected, his mother knew a hell of a lot more than she was saying. They watched her. At the same time they discouraged local parents from forming vigilante groups.

At this level the case of the missing boy Sam Wylie was ordinary enough. Children do go missing, and they are either found dead or discovered alive, somewhere.

There is a straightforward explanation even if you never find the criminal. The disappearance of Sam had deeper roots, and went further back in time. Thus, it was not a picture of the crime that the police needed, but something more like a holograph with all parts moving freely in space and time.

Harry Shaw, who was the editor of the *Lukesfield Herald*, and who also owned the paper, had realised for himself that stories about missing children sold newspapers; he had a word with his chief reporter which was the most sensible thing he did that day, since afterwards he went home and beat his wife. He did not use the word beat, even to himself, naturally, thinking of it as a rightful explosion of anger which she had richly deserved. She had long since learnt to take her own precautions and the beating did not cause her any undue discomfort.

Joe Archibald, the reporter, who was a stringer for several London newspapers, including the *Daily Telegraph*, was also a writer, and man of feeling.

'Stay with that story,' his boss had commanded. 'I want us to find the boy. Or be there when he is found.'

A steep order, Joe Archibald felt. 'The police will be doing that.'

'Not necessarily. I don't think he was kidnapped. I think he went. Use your imagination. Be with him, *be* that boy. Get into his mind.'

'I'm not God.'

'Act as if you were.'

Joe thought about it. 'And if the boy is dead?'

'God would know about it first too, wouldn't he?'

At this point his editor had looked harassed. 'Now push off. I've got some work to see to. . . . Get the article in by Thursday to appear this weekend.'

This was on top of Joe's ordinary routine, naturally, which this week involved interviewing the local MP, also a feature on a rat-catcher who was being evicted from his tied cottage because an animal protection society had bought the estate, and several brides about to be married with much fuss and expense.

'Can I take Sandy?'

Sandy was the photographer.

'Half a day only. I want him for the rest of the day. God knows he works slowly enough.'

Joe reflected that even half a day of Sandy might be worth it: he was such a marvellous man for noticing important details. His photographs were competent, no more, but his observation of life was acute. He might pick up just the detail which led to Sam and which would show in the photograph.

Joe would have followed up the story of Sam in any case because he found it absorbing, almost obsessional. As he walked about the streets of Lukesfield he had found himself thinking: Is he in that house, shut into a cupboard? Behind that garage door? Fallen into that gravel pit and unable to get out?

These were the more cheerful, positive daytime thoughts. The second night of Sam's disappearance, as he walked his dog in the shrubby area of the gravel pits he wondered if the dog's sniffing around might dig up the boy's body. The dog was a liver-coloured mongrel called Lucifer.

Lucifer turned nothing up. It would have been surprising if he had, because Joe knew that the whole area had been sectioned off and searched by the police several days earlier. Local people had stood in their windows staring, or had turned away feeling sick. Maggie was one of those who had looked and felt sick. At Pettit's School all the blinds were drawn on that side of the school building, while old Miss Pettit, indomitable as ever, read aloud a Richmal Crompton story about William and his Outlaws. The children knew about Sam's disappearance, but maintained a reserve on the subject. His name was not mentioned, but perhaps they talked about him when they believed the adults were not listening. Miss Pettit, for one, thought that they did, and she was trying to listen, but so far had picked up nothing of interest. She was only one of a number of listeners, because Maggie was eavesdropping as the High-Lo gang cleaned the windows, while Ellen who came to the school daily to see Tom was listening, too. Biddy Powell herself, on instructions from the police, was overhearing what she could. It struck her that the children were being remarkably quiet, remarkably reserved. She had never thought of her pupils as a taciturn bunch but they seemed so now. For a group of highly sophisticated, highly articulate kids they suddenly seemed to have little to say for themselves.

But she continued listening; as did Maggie; as did Ellen, and as Joe was to do.

Joe had already spoken to Ellen, he had not needed prompting from his editor to that end. She was approachable enough. Get her in the right mood and Ellen would talk. She had talked to him, weeping but coherent, and he had believed her tale. She had carried conviction. To him, he thought, she had spoken the truth. More of the truth than to the police, anyway.

He called at her home, Oakwood, with Sandy. Sandy had taken some photographs, then departed leaving Joe to carry on. He would have a go later at photographing the school. On his own, please, because that way he got better pictures.

'There's nothing you're not telling me?' Joe had asked.

'Nothing.' Ellen's eyes were blue and clouded; he thought she was the loveliest thing he had ever seen. He was always to think that. He even liked her faint air of dissipation. It brought out the evangelist in him, made him feel that there was a soul worth saving. 'Surely you believe me?'

Yes, he believed her, but still it wasn't an entirely believable story she told, with the details so sparse.

'Let me have it again, please,' he had said, deliberately putting on his best reporter's manner to calm her down, almost trying to make a joke of it. 'You realised at once that Sam wasn't there: you looked for him. He wasn't in the house. You thought you had left his bedroom door locked, but the door was open and so was the door from the kitchen to the garden. He was gone. And you have no idea where or with whom. Or even if with anyone.'

Such was Ellen's tale, the story that everyone knew.

One extra detail he knew and no one else. Not Nicholas, not Maggie, probably not the police.

Maggie knew that Ellen had left Sam locked in his room for a longer time than she was admitting and that she had done it before.

Nicholas knew that Ellen beat Sam. Not often, but sometimes.

Joe Archibald knew that what Ellen did was to give her son a sedative, and he knew this, not because she had told him, but because it was what his own mother had done to him as a child.

Of course he did not know what drug Ellen used or what its effects on Sam were, but he could guess: Sam would not have been exactly legless but relaxed and easy so that anyone could have taken him anywhere.

So that was what Joe Archibald knew that no one else did.

Eventually he made his way to Pettit's School, as a starting place for his enquiry, as suggested by his editor. He had worked out that the time to listen to the children was when they were at play. But Biddy had already thought of this, and the children played indoors that day, so he wasted his time then. However, at dinner time they all came piling out and it was less easy to control them. He was hanging about again then, looking for an entry point.

In the interval he had covered other stories and attended to a few details of personal matters, including looking in on his own home. He had some small private life of his own, he called it small, others might have called it free, active and far ranging. Most of this life was conducted from his caravan home. A truly mobile home suited him because he liked to shift his headquarters. Sometimes he parked in one place, sometimes in another. At the moment he was based just out of Lukesfield, facing towards the industrial belt that made a half circle around its northern perimeter. He felt comfortable here; it was neither town nor country, neither one thing nor another which was how he saw himself: he was a nowhere man.

The children were milling around. The school was small, but the highly privileged well-fed pupils were preternaturally active and exceptionally noisy. Hard to put down.

Ellen was waiting to see Tom. She turned up every day now to sit beside him while he ate. It posed a real problem for Biddy who did not want her there, but could not see how to keep her out.

Joe and Ellen recognised each other.

'Hi Joe,' said Ellen in a toneless voice. A look passed between them. Joe had the same feeling about Ellen that Nicholas had: that if he shook her hard then some small nugget of information about Sam might drop out. But, unlike Nicholas, he guessed that Ellen could lie under pressure and that what popped out might not be the truth.

Even a lie might be useful, though. Some people's lies tell more of the truth than they guess, more than their truth.

There was a lie in her look now, and one in his gaze back.

He bowed slightly to her as if she was a widow in mourning, which was how he thought of her, somehow. She moved a hand slightly in reply before going on to find Tom.

Miss Pettit's School was housed in a large, plain building which had once been a private house. It had been well adapted to serve as a school some fifty years ago when Miss Pettit came into her inheritance. Before this her school had been based in a few huts, left over from the First World War. Pettit's was now at its popular, fashionable peak. Parents fought to enrol their children there so they could get them into the brown, canary yellow and white uniform as soon as they could toddle. Girls stayed until they were twelve, before going on somewhere smart like Bedales or Heathfield, boys left about the same time for the better public schools. Joe, who had already interviewed Biddy, had not tried to get any words with Miss Pettit, because he knew it would be no go. It was like trying to interview the Queen: you couldn't do it just for the asking.

Biddy, who was watching the children run around, saw Joe and shook her head. 'No more to say.'

'My paper wants to help find Sam. *I* want to help.'

'Nevertheless . . . ' Biddy knew that the school was sharing the limelight with Ellen, but she maintained a careful and dignified silence.

They were both watching Ellen. She put her arm round Tom, then together the two of them walked into the school, Tom to eat his lunch, Ellen to watch him. Ellen did not eat, perhaps was not eating much at all these days.

'Sorry to have bothered you, Mrs Powell.' He acted as if he was going away, but in fact he strolled off in the direction of the gravel pits, which curved around the school, making for a point in the fence through which he could observe and listen to the children when they came out to play after eating. The gravel-pit wasteland was jagged with rough bushes and catches of bramble, but rough little tracks crossed it, and he knew his way. He had the map of it in his mind.

Maggie and Evadne, having washed about half the windows, inside and out, were eating their lunch in company with two young teachers. They both saw Ellen come in with Tom, and from her seat by the window Maggie also saw Joe Archibald in his conversation with Biddy, and her gaze became thoughtful. She thought she'd seen him before.

Biddy slipped into her place and started eating cheese salad. She ate what the children ate to encourage them. Maggie poured her a glass of water.

'Hello.' Biddy sought for conversation on any subject other than the one that interested them most. 'How are you getting on with the hypnotism?'

'Fine. He's got me off smoking.'

'Are you on to something else?'

It sometimes happened that, after being cured of one addiction, you straightaway fell into another.

'Not so I've noticed,' said Maggie cautiously. 'But you never know what's round the next corner.' It might be that David was her new addiction. Or it might be the way she kept seeing blood. 'How's he doing with Mary's hay fever?'

'She's stopped sniffing.' Biddy chewed resolutely on a tough piece of lettuce. 'But she's taken up sleep-walking.'

The two women, who were friends, looked at each other with sympathy.

'Tension?' said Maggie.

'Possible.'

'Can you blame her? I wonder all the children aren't affected.'

'Oh, they are. In their own way. It just takes them differently. They're as jumpy as little cats. Noisy, yet quiet in an odd way. The don't talk about *it*, you know. Not a word. Or if they do then they take care I don't hear.'

Across the room Tom had finished his meal and was rising to go; Ellen with him. At no time had he addressed a word to his mother. Ellen had not said much, but she had tried. Now she followed him from the room in a docile fashion.

Biddy shook her head slightly. 'He won't speak to her, did you notice that? It was the same yesterday.'

Tom had hardly looked at his mother, just chewed his food fast, as if he liked food, was determined to have it, but wanted to get it over with.

Maggie said, 'Do you think he's still alive?' She didn't have to name names. Sam.

Biddy shrugged. 'Don't know. I hope so. Do you think Ellen *knows*? Somehow I feel that she does. Has she said anything to you? She trusts you. You're closer to her than almost anyone.'

'Nothing to quote.'

'Then she has.'

'No, I don't mean it that way. I mean she's miserable and confused.'

To her surprise Biddy accepted her defence of Ellen peacefully, perhaps with relief. 'Exactly how I feel myself.'

'There you are then. How's Mary taking it? Apart from the sleep-walking.'

'Calmly, and in her own way. There's more going on under the surface than she lets me know, but I'll deal with that when it surfaces.'

It was a wise mother that knew its own child, thought Maggie as she finished her meal. She could see Mary chatting away to her friends with her usual decorum. An exceptionally nice child, as befitted Biddy's daughter. Her father now, that had been another matter, but that *was* another matter. But that was also long ago and over and done with. Mary wouldn't know about it.

One of the young teachers called across to Biddy, 'Could you come, please, Mrs Powell?' and Biddy, as she rose to go, whispered to Maggie: 'There's a journalist about. He's trying to speak to the children. Just a warning.'

So that's who he is, thought Maggie. I knew I'd seen him before. It was at the Garden Club dance. He was there taking notes.... He had been there with a pretty blonde, too. Obviously one for the girls.... And hadn't Ellen been there and danced with him? That might be an illusion, though, as Maggie seemed to see Ellen everywhere at the moment.

Evadne had already returned to work, conscientious as ever. Maggie took her bucket and went out into the play area to wipe down the Wendy House. As a playing centre this house had its ups and downs, sometimes yielding place in popularity stakes to the slide, sometimes to the toy grocery-shop which sold pretend tins of soup and beans with painted pots of jam and wooden biscuits. It was the prototype for the one the children had built at Oakwood.

Lately the Wendy House had been top among one set, and the slide among the other. The little shop was, as far as Maggie could see, at present totally neglected. Someone had roughed it up a bit, but that was all.

She could see a group of children in the Wendy House now. Just the tops of their heads were visible through the window, impossible to see who they were.

She strolled that way, driven by a strong curiosity. It was sneaky, listening to children at play, but justified in the circumstances.

Loud, clear, cheerful voices sounded. Two children at least were talking and another chipping in. As she watched a small boy hurried out of the door to run across the playground. His brown and yellow overall was unbuttoned, flapping so that he looked like a little yellow bird.

A voice from inside the Wendy House summoned him back.

Mary Powell, decided Maggie, and well in command, too, judging by the tone.

The boy wheeled round and disappeared into the little house, presently to reappear with his overall buttoned, hair sleeked down and cheeks red as if polished.

Mary tidied him up. The maternal instinct must run strong there.

'Hello,' said Maggie, as he came skipping past. 'Who are you?'

'Slightly.'

'Slighly what?'

'Just slightly,' he said with a giggle and ran off.

Presently another little boy squeezed his way out of the house. He was flushed and damp round the cheeks and eyes as if he had been crying.

'Are you all right?'

He looked up at Maggie in surprise. 'Yes, course.'

'You've been crying.'

'Yes. It's my turn to cry. . . . I'm best at it,' he said proudly.

Funny game, thought Maggie, but no doubt in the game of Mothers and Fathers, mothers must chastise and children must cry. She started to make adult noises of sympathy, just in case.

But the crying boy had walked away.

Meanwhile the Wendy House was having a spring-clean. Maggie could see the windows being washed. Yes, it was Mary Powell at work.

She rapped on the door. The voices inside were still going at it.

'Never,' said Mary Powell, then she said it again: Never, never.

Maggie banged on the door again.

'Not at home,' called a voice. Tom's voice, she thought. 'Gone away.' There was the sound of giggling.

Biddy Powell appeared at the school door with a small handbell which she rang vigorously. Playtime was over.

Inside the house Tom and Mary heard the bell also. They smiled at each other, having enjoyed their game. Mary took it seriously. To her it was hardly a game. The impulse too serious, chastising motherhood was very strong in her. Instinctively she was aware that Mother Knew Best. Tom accepted her part: he had his own role to play.

The childish voices rose in a chant. 'Never,' they intoned, 'never, never.'

The house was equipped with a table and chairs of a small sort, together with a wooden frame bed. A wooden cupboard stretched across one wall, its shelves filled with toy cooking utensils such as saucepans and frying pans. They were of good quality, but battered with use. A larder in the wall held a supply of food, most of it pretend cakes, bread and fruit, but some of it real, apples and nuts.

Mary-Wendy checked her supplies with satisfaction. She had enough for today. Tomorrow would always be within her power to cope with. It always had been. The reality in which she lived was intense and luminous.

Hand in hand Tom and Mary left the play house in response to Biddy's bell. Maggie followed them.

Joe Archibald, taking his own way and his own time, had got through the rough lands of the gravel pits and had arrived at the belt of trees that fringed Pettit's School. These trees were part of a new plantation which had been established to take the place of those killed at the time of the acid rain. They were conifers chosen for their power to grow fast; they were doing their best, but the soil offered little support, perhaps even a downright hindrance. The fir trees, thin and scrawny, lined up with the open scrub around the deserted pits. It was amazing how that land stretched out its tentacles.

Trees don't walk, don't watch and can't stare, Joe told himself, the universal laws preclude it, but at times like this he felt these trees did. They were, with the exception of the prosperous old oak, lean and hungry trees such as Caesar might have abhorred. Let me have trees about me that are stout, he told himself, yon trees have a desolate air on them as if their juices were sucked by some monstrous lips.

As an ecologist he had sympathy with trees, but just now he felt it would be nice if the trees had sympathy back.

Joe was a sensitive man, inclined to such thoughts, almost ready to invent them if they did not arrive on time.

He arrived at the belt of trees near the Wendy House in time to watch the insertion of at least four children into the little place and the arrival of Maggie. He knew Maggie, and unlike Maggie who had got it all wrong and thought it was at a dance (although there was a dance in his mind so perhaps she had picked up this thought) he knew it was at the dentist's that they had met. In the waiting room.

He had poor teeth but a splendid God-given visual memory. He liked the look of Maggie, a lovely, warm attractive lady.

He saw all that Maggie saw, but placed a different interpretation on it. Those kids are up to no good, he told himself. He was, in some ways, a harsher and more realistic critic of life than Maggie.

He saw Tom and Mary come out of the little house, hand in hand, closing the door behind them with care. The care was Mary's, Tom only watched.

Maggie followed them.

Suddenly Mary turned round, still holding Tom by the hand, and spoke to Maggie, glancing briefly at Joe as she did so. Their eyes met. Joe drew in a harsh breath as if a pain had started.

It was a harsh, grating pain as if the bones of hip and leg were stretching. Splitting. The pain spread, chewing into his innards, sharp, ragged, bloody, like a saw-edged knife cutting into him.

He staggered back against a tree.

I don't believe this, he told himself, I am going to die, and it is not my time to die. He tried to pray.

Then it was over. Creaking, stretching, the pain was gone. It hadn't lasted more than a second.

Imagination? Or a twitch of the nervous system such as we all get occasionally.

He had the strange feeling that he was picking up a set of sensations from Maggie. He was feeling a pain that he knew was not his pain or even a real pain, all the same it was ferocious.

What remained was anger. A great anger was burning inside him. The anger blotting out even the pain. He was furiously, monstrously angry, angry like a devil, like a god, like an immortal.

The children went out of sight into the school. The pain went away, the anger faded.

Joe drew a deep breath, he was whole again, his own man. That was a bloody business, he thought.

I've been crucified, a voice inside his head said, so that he looked at his hands to see if there was a stigmata. Nothing there, his hands were clear.

Maggie had seen him and was hurrying across to speak to him. 'Please go away,' she said in a fierce voice. 'Go away and leave the children alone. I'm a friend of Ellen Wylie. Leave her alone.'

'I like her myself.' His voice was mild, and it was true: he did like Ellen.

'Well, just go.'

'I won't write anything unpleasant. I want to help, to find the boy.' His earnestness and truthfulness got through to Maggie. 'Won't you help me?'

'I'll tell you one thing. Or perhaps it's a series of things. . . . He had chances of being on his own. . . . I don't want to go into that but I know it was so.'

Joe nodded: he knew it also: Ellen's little leaving ways.

Maggie went on. 'I think Sam may have taken his freedom. He wasn't a dull boy, you know. Shut up in himself, inarticulate, yes, but not stupid. Of that I'm sure. He had ideas of his own. Why not ask if anyone ever saw him around on his own?'

'That's a good idea.' She was beautiful and good, thought Joe. A woman to whom you could put difficult questions, a woman to talk to.

Another channel of communication had been opened: all channels were now open and running free.

He considered going home to bed, but in his present state of shock it would have felt like a sepulchre. First thing tomorrow he would move the bus. A change of scene would benefit him. He would move more into the heart of Lukesfield. Nearer to Ellen, nearer to Maggie, nearer to the school.

He was the investigator, the innocent eye, the man who

would see. He was something else as well, but he was finding it increasingly difficult to put a name to what that was.

He went to the public library for a rest. It was one of his private places of call. He had learnt how to make best use of it. There was a small corner in the reference library, underneath the new *Encyclopaedia Britannica* where no one ever came and where you could have a quiet God's pause if you felt like it. He called it that.

Not today, though. He took the first seat he could find and began his deep-breathing exercises which were supposed to calm him down. While he breathed he tried to form a picture of what had happened to Sam and where he might be.

He couldn't make up his mind if the children knew anything or not. They were playing it deep if they did. But apparently children could. So they might have an idea where Sam was to be found. If found he ever was. Ellen on the other hand was totally at sea; he believed her on that one.

So what had he got?

A boy taken from his home because his mother fancied a quiet hour or two. Probably drugged in a mild kind of way by his mother, and therefore passive. From this he deduced that whoever had taken Sam, or, if you looked at it in another way, had helped Sam away, had known of Ellen's habits. If this person knew Ellen that well, then that same person probably knew Sam.

That needed a bit of thinking about, didn't it? A friend? A relation? Not so many of either around, so your choice was limited.

He sighed. Not brilliant, not brilliant at all, but he was getting on.

There was a coffee machine in the lobby not far from where he was sitting, next to the Space-Invader electronic box which was supposed to bring some money into the library funds while satisfying the junior readers. It did not. The young taste had moved on, and found the game dull. Books were better.

Joe went over and got himself some coffee, which was black and reasonably hot, then sat drinking it as he made notes for his article.

Presently the librarian came up and took his beaker of coffee away. 'You're not doing any good with that. Come and have a cup of the real stuff in my office.'

'Glad to.' She was a coffee maker of distinction. Good coffee was a way to his heart (not his soul, he kept that in a different place) as she knew well. It had been her idea that he had a *bad* heart, he sometimes looked so tired, perhaps a smaller one than normal, which needed to be 'perked up' by strong coffee, but she had abandoned this idea as whimsical.

'You look rotten.'

'I've had a shock. No, not a shock. . . . Pain. A great wave of it. Gone now but I can still remember it. They say you don't remember pain, but I can.'

'That's labour pains with women, I think.'

'Felt like that. My whole body was on the rack.' He gave a shudder. 'And I felt so angry. A terrible anger.'

She was concerned. 'Are you sure you are all right? What about seeing a doctor?'

'I will do if it comes back.' But could you have a doctor for anger? And the anger had been the pain and the pain the anger, the two were one. Pain was the ideal habitat for anger. He had the nasty idea that it might be a growing thing and that next time the pain-anger might be greater.

'It's the missing boy,' said Miss Lavender wisely. 'We're all in a state. I've had indigestion ever since I heard. And I was frightened to walk home alone last night.'

She poured out two cups of coffee, added cream and opened a tin of home-made biscuits.

He drank gratefully. 'You know the boy, do you?'

'I know the whole family. Mother, father, and the two boys. They used to be in and out at one time. Not that Sam can read, but he looks at pictures. The library seemed to soothe him down. He took a lot in, I always thought.'

'Pettit's School come in as a group, don't they?'

'They certainly do. Great little readers. Everything from Lamb's *Tales from Shakespeare* and Sir James Barrie to Enid Blyton. Biddy doesn't control what they read, lets them choose for themselves, says that's part of reading. So it is. Of course,

Miss Pettit likes to weigh in on behalf of the classics as she calls them. Something in that too,' she said tolerantly. As long as people read, used her books, showed appreciation, she was on their side.

She was sipping her coffee and busy putting together a file of papers. One fluttered out, he picked it up to return to her. 'This your Local History Group? Are you reading a paper?' He had attended himself once or twice. Not really interested, but impelled somehow to go.

'It meets tonight. No, I'm not reading a paper. Our leader is doing it tonight. Why don't you come? Take you out of yourself.'

For some reason the phrase gave him the shakes. Out of himself, turned inside out, innards to the outside. Oh, that was a nasty picture.

'I have a meeting of my own tonight. I might look in later.'

'Oh yes, that's right . . . would have come but for this. . . . I'd forgotten for the moment it was your night for saving the world.'

'Well, cleaning it up,' he said stiffly. 'Saving it might be a tall order. I might come in to you later.' Ecology, for him, was a religion. He was deeply preoccupied with pollution and threats like acid rain. Sometimes he walked round the gravel-pit area and commiserated with the sad trees and shrubs. He made it a personal message. The big oak tree which flourished so strongly and strangely struck him as not needing any such attention, having its own arrogant assertion of life. He disliked the tree, in fact, surprised that any member of the vegetable world could provoke such a response. Perhaps the tree had Sam.

Another nasty thought. Where were they all coming from? He remembered something he had to ask. 'Have you ever seen Sam around on his own?'

'Funny you should ask that.' Her tone was respectful; she did respect Joe, she thought he had powers. 'I have. I saw Sam Wylie running through the streets one afternoon, skipping about, laughing and waving his arms about as if he was flying.'

'Once?'

'Twice.'

'Any idea where he was going?'

She laughed and shook her head. 'I don't know. Where do all the birds go when they fly? To the trees.'

Echo answers to echo.

The Local History Group were going to meet on this evening on which Joe Archibald wrote up his day's report, not mentioning Sam's running-flying through the streets of Lukesfield. Joe then went to his own ecology meeting, which was sparsely attended and so he still had time to look in on the Local History Group which exercised a certain pull over him.

They had reached the Post-Reformation period, when Protestant Elizabeth had succeeded her sister Catholic Queen Mary and then been succeeded in her turn by Scottish James. This had been a time of some violence in England, a violence which had also washed over the quiet little hamlet of St Lukes Field.

There had been one particularly unpleasant martyrdom, of which the last scenes had been played out in St Lukes Field. Whether you thought of it as a martyrdom or the justifiable hanging, drawing and quartering of a traitor to the King's Peace, depended on which side of the religious divide you stood.

The local dentist was leading the discussion. He had in his briefcase an edited version taken from a contemporary account of the full and horrible details of the execution of Martha Littlebody who had plotted to kill the monarch by poison. This account had been edited in 1919 by his grandfather, also a dentist. An edition of this book was deposited in the library, and although it was a nasty story, was on the open shelves and freely available.

His grandfather had been fascinated by the story, identifying strongly with the details of Martha's execution. He had made a black joke. 'Littlebody, so called,' he had said, 'but they stretched that little body.' She was racked, hung, drawn and quartered. In the process a hand came off and was lost.

And within that Littlebody was another little body, but that was not his joke, only nature's.

There were circles interlocking down the years; the dentist liked to think that a remote ancestor of his own had lived here when Martha Littlebody came back to be buried. His grandpa had certainly primed him to believe this. He himself had gone to Pettit's School and been taught by Miss Pettit, and much influenced by her. She could do that when she chose. 'Mind. Spirit. Imagination,' those were her keywords. 'Use the imagination.'

Nicholas and Ellen had once been members of this group. Nicholas thought you should know about where you lived, it gave a depth and solidity to your life. He hardly remembered his own father, and his grandparents not at all, so it was very necessary to him to thicken his own shadow. Ellen had no sense of wanting to know anyone's past, but probably took more in because she listened while Nicholas made careful notes and was thus too busy to listen.

The Wylies were not present that night.

At the end of the day Maggie made her report. To herself because there was no one else around. She said:

I listened to the children. There was no talk about Sam at first. Not while I was around. I felt they did not want to talk. . . . Or be overheard talking about Sam. There was a holding back . . . but I must remember that they are just children.

But it would be more natural for children to talk, even to say whatever they thought I wanted them to say. Perhaps I don't know enough about children.

I walked around the garden after I had finished cleaning the Wendy House. . . . I don't like that little house, I think it's got dry rot, I must tell Biddy. The garden was a wreck. Been pretty once, but absolutely battered to bits by the children. Childish feet have trampled over the plants without caring. Suddenly I came to see that children could be very cruel. I could admire these self-absorbed, ruthless creatures but they frightened me.

I am not a child lover. Looking at Biddy at the end of the afternoon I saw that neither was she. She respected them, but that is another thing altogether.

Children, like the rich, are different. . . . If you scratch them, do they not bleed? Well, I wonder.

I heard one thing. I heard one child say that perhaps Sam was

shut in the drawer. That child giggled as he spoke.
What drawer?
Perhaps I misheard.

Later that day, having completed their reports, Joe Archibald and Maggie both went, feeling impelled somehow, to the Local History Group. It was something to do, and would take the mind off current worries. The motive was much the same in both cases. Maggie had tried unsuccessfully to get Ellen to go to stay with her mother, but Ellen had gone back to Oakwood. Nicholas was still with his mother who was looking after Tom. David was working. Biddy took a sleeping tablet and went to bed early, first looking in on her peacefully dreaming child.
Sam slept.
Across the room at the meeting in the library, Maggie and Joe looked at each other. She was feeling pretty good, having had no migraines lately. On the other hand, he had a bad, frontal headache.

Chapter Four

Across the room the eyes of Joe and Maggie met, a spark, no more, but sufficient, passed between them. They were surprised at the attraction, and surprised to see each other. It was the first time they had met at the Local History Group. It made a link between them. There were other links too, although, except for the Ellen-Sam knot, they were not apparent to them at the time. Nor to anyone else.

Maggie registered the attraction, and put it aside for future inspection.

Before coming to the group, she had cooked a meal for Ellen and stayed with her while she ate it. It was like feeding a little bird, you had to push the spoonfuls almost into her mouth.

It had been her intention not to ask questions, but one popped out before she could stop it. She thought she knew what Ellen was up to when she locked Sam in his room, and taking a turn in the fresh air was not it.

'You've got a lover, haven't you?' Probably more than one, but one special one. 'Someone who used to visit you at home, and whom you're keeping quiet about.'

'Don't. Please don't, Maggie. Don't you see I've had enough questions?'

Maggie pressed on. 'And that's what you were doing when Sam was supposed to be locked in his room. Making love. In your bedroom. Come on, you might as well say. I'm not shocked.'

Ellen kept quiet.

'Why aren't you saying? Why protect him, Ellen? If he came forward he might get you out of a spot.'

'Put me in one you mean. . . . I can just see that detective's face, No, thank you. Besides, he's a *good* person. I don't want to drag him into this.'

'He could prove you knew nothing about Sam going. Say how surprised you were.' . . . Or he could testify that you were guilty. You might both be guilty. That was the obverse side of the question, as Ellen had shrewdly pointed out. Not such a fool this girl.

'Do I know him?' Maggie had asked.

'No. Certainly not.'

The remark was delivered like a slap in the face. Ellen was certainly a hard person to help.

'I had to have someone. I have needs like other people. *You* ought to understand. I'm not in love. What's love? That's what Nicholas and I had. I don't believe in that any more. I'm Sam's shadow and his keeper, but I have to have my times off.'

'Did Nicholas know?'

'Of course not. No one knew.'

But Sam knew; Sam might have seen more than he should, and Sam, after his outburst at the party (whatever he had said, whatever he had poured out), could now no longer be trusted to be silent. He could talk. It was a motive for getting rid of Sam.

From her pocket Maggie drew Sam's yellow submarine, carefully wrapped in a plastic bag so that her hands need not touch it.

'Here you are. You left this behind.'

'Oh good, I thought I'd lost it. It might help me find Sam like it did before—' She stopped.

'You might as well go on.' How many times had Ellen 'lost' Sam?

'Once or twice he has got out. . . . ' Ellen made him sound like a dog. Or a bird. 'He used to think he could fly. . . . When it happened once before I went out into the road and did this.' She put the yellow submarine to her lips. 'It may look like a boat but it's a whistle. I blew and he came running.'

She blew on the tin whistle and a sharp thin sound came out, a noise like vinegar, a sound to scrape the ears. Maggie winced.

Ellen had stopped blowing. Her pretty, expressionless little mask anchored into position as usual.

The doorbell had rung.

'That's the police. Or Nick with his lawyer. Both call every day to look me over. To see if I have got Sam here. Or am burying him. Or eating him. I am very thoroughly inspected.'

'And you won't say about this man?'

Suddenly Ellen smiled. 'Oh I'll *tell* you, Maggie. He's called Charley Soul.'

Maggie frowned. 'Don't I know the name? Who is he? Where did you meet him?'

'He runs a Life Class. You know, to teach you to be a better person. Perhaps you think I don't need that.' The delightful smile that had once attracted Nicholas lightened her face. She looked young, happy. 'But then he is lovely looking and I've always been a sucker for looks. That's how Nicholas got me. I never could resist how he looked.'

Seeing Ellen's face like that somehow made you understand what Ophelia had got herself into.

Maggie let herself out at the front door. It was Nicholas arriving. They did not speak. Sam was not found.

All the time that Maggie was listening to Arthur Chamberlain read his paper, she was also listening to the sound of the yellow submarine. It was beginning to make her head ache again, and as her head ached the whistle seemed to change into a thin scream of animal pain. A female animal. How can a cry of pain have a sex? But it appeared that it could have.

Maggie listened dutifully but without much interest to what Mr Chamberlain had to say. He was talking about the lists of death recorded in Lukesfield parish records of the sixteenth century, when it had still been called St Lukes Field. He pointed out that St Luke was the patron saint of madmen. Then be began reading long lists of names and dates of the dead. He had a dull, monotonous delivery. Maggie felt as though she had heard it all before. He made you feel like that.

Over coffee afterwards she found herself standing, not entirely by chance, next to Joe Archibald.

'Not a natural performer,' he said looking towards Arthur Chamberlain.

'No, it's amazing how numbers keep up in the group. I don't know why we all keep coming. I didn't really mean to do so tonight, but I somehow felt obliged to. Haven't I heard it all once before, though?'

'Spontaneous with me, too. I just found myself coming. I still don't know why. What's the history of St Lukes Field to me?'

'Miss Lavender likes it.'

The librarian was talking with animation to Mr Chamberlain.

'Yes, she's a real addict.'

'Not only her.'

It was indeed a crowded room, Arthur certainly knew how to hang on to his audience. Joe had already seen his boss and editor sitting at the back of the room with the exhausted air of one who hadn't meant to be there, but somehow was. He recognised a sprinkling of others as well: Teddy Gray the local plumber, Frank Middleway and his wife (she had to be his wife, but she looked young enough to be his daughter) who had the franchise for the local hamburger take-away, Alison Pritt, from the typing agency by the railway station, and a local writer, a woman. There were plenty of faces he did not recognise, too. A mixed collection to have turned up and to be so docile and ready to listen. Most of them looked as though they would have been happier at home watching TV. Representatives of the commuting-to-London set were there also, grouped together trying to look as if local history was their interest of the month.

'I was a bit rough on you this afternoon. Sorry.'

'No need. When I'm doing a job like that I know what to expect. . . . May I introduce myself: Joe Archibald.'

'Maggie Chase.'

'I know. Nice name. Mine makes me sound like a wife murderer, someone who ought to appear in the *News of the World*. My mother wanted to call me Peter. I'm glad I missed that too.'

'You are in a rotten mood.'

'And unmarried, may I say. This coffee is lousy. Come and have a drink. I want to talk to you.'

Maggie hesitated, then said, 'Love to. What do we talk about?'

'The boy. I think those kids know where he is.'

'I think *some* of them know *something*,' amended Maggie. 'I'm not sure if they know where he is. Perhaps it's just a game they are playing.'

Lukesfield had two pubs, the Dreadnought Gun and the Barley Mow, and one wine-bar called Penny's Pound.

Joe and Maggie went to the wine-bar. Maggie selected it because she had gone to the Gun with her husband, and sometimes to the Barley Mow with David. Joe chose the wine-bar because he was sensitive to Maggie's mind and felt this was what she preferred.

Over red wine, mulled because the evening had turned chilly, he said, 'How do you get on with the children at Pettit's. . . . Do they like you?'

'Normally. I'm not sure if I like children. I think they frighten me at times. But I passionately regret that I have not had one. So I listen to them and take them in.'

Ellen was a sort of child, so had her husband been. Not David. Nor this man with her now. They were adult. She had never been quite so explicit before; she surprised herself. But he seemed to understand.

'Would they talk to you? Tell you things that were otherwise secret?'

'No, probably not. . . .' She considered. 'They aren't very old. I expect I could get something out of them. Pick something up.'

'Clues.'

'If one can use that word – I don't think even the police use it much now.' David did not. Information received, hard facts, positive indications, that was the way he talked. He had told her the police did not know much. He had not told her what they thought. 'But why should I help you?'

'Because I want to find the boy – all right, it's for ambitious reasons. It would *make* me. And you have your own reasons. Together we can do more than one alone.'

'So?'

'He's been around, you know, on his own. Been seen. That lad had his moments of freedom.'

'Yes, I know. Ellen told me,' she admitted.

'Well, he went *somewhere.*'

He passed a photograph across the table to her. The picture was of Ellen and Tom, the latter with head averted apparently, staring into the distance, away from his mother. Sandy had taken it.

'What does that mean to you?'

Maggie looked. 'He's miserable. Ellen's wretched. That's what it means.'

'It's a picture of a boy who knows something. And look in the background.' He pointed. Trees, shrubs, the Wendy House. At the window of the Wendy House, a face, just visible. 'And notice what the boy's looking at. There's a kid at the window watching, who is that?'

'I don't know.' The face was a blur. 'Why?'

He studied the photograph. 'Might be important. That little play house – a sort of meeting place, isn't it?'

'The Wendy House?'

That particular group of children, Tom and Mary and Co, were obsessed with houses, Maggie had noticed.

'That's what it's called?' He packed the photograph away. 'You don't think Sam could be in it?'

'The police must have thought of it, must have looked.'

'All the same. . . . I can't get in and look. But you could.'

Maggie was silent. It felt like betraying a lot of people. But to what? Or to whom?

'You don't like the idea?'

'No.'

'Why not?'

'Frightens me. Silly, I suppose. I don't know what I'll find.'

Sam couldn't be in the Wendy House, could he?' If he was, then all the children (or some of them) knew and were keeping quiet, his own brother Tom, and Mary Powell included.

No, it was impossible. It could not be.

'All the same, worth a look.' He was persuasive, as only Joe knew how.

They finished their wine, drank some more coffee. Allies at last. He established the existence of her missing husband, flushed out the existence of David about whom Maggie now had guilt feelings. Her brush with Ellen had made her ask if she was using sex with him as therapy, and the answer had to be that, yes, to a certain extent, she was. For her part, she had found out that Joe was unmarried, orphaned, and keen on ecology.

Maggie ended up with an uneasy feeling that something was coming free, struggling out of the ground, arms like roots, legs knotted and earthy. She was alarmed at her own imagery.

They made arrangements to keep in touch and pass on information. A process not without difficulty since Joe could only be telephoned at his offices. He'd always ring back if he was out, though. That was how they left it.

Arthur Chamberlain, Dental Surgeon, had noticed Maggie and Joe depart together. He admired Maggie, so usually kept an eye out for her. His deepest preoccupations were with the history of Lukesfield and with the practice of anaesthesia; Maggie slotted into both, somewhere.

His wife Dorothy made them a pot of tea as soon as they got home, together with a plate of sandwiches. 'I don't think I shall come to the next meeting, dear. I feel as though I know enough local history.'

'If that's how you feel, Dolly.' He was unconcerned; he had his loyal band of listeners who would not desert him. Dolly never had been one.

After thirty years of marriage Dolly thought this *was* how she felt. She marvelled how his class held together, but it did. People dropped out, but others came. She had wondered sometimes if people moved house so they *could* leave. The Chamberlains had never moved, had lived for generations in the same area in Lukesfield, but Dolly came from Rotherford Royal across the county.

'Excellent sandwiches, love. By the way, this coming week I shall be over to Abbotsford General for a meeting of the DHA planning committee – we're discussing the layout of the new mental hospital. It's going through about siting it here. The new chap's coming over to speak to us about it. Sort of a public relations exercise. There's always that side to it.' He took another sandwich. 'Did you make this pâté yourself?'

'Bought it from Luckam's.'

Luckam's was the Fortnum and Mason's of Lukesfield. Dolly stood up, brushing crumbs from her lap. 'I'm going to bed. Don't stay up too late, dear.' She touched his shoulder fondly. She knew what a proud man he was, and she always wanted to protect him from that pride. To say: Look dear, it doesn't matter. Forget it.

It was good of him to be so welcoming to the asylum. Was it a front, a kind of shield? It was a case for watching out. Things did wind up so. Hubble, bubble, toil and trouble. She had been a good amateur Shakespearian once (before the 'trouble' time, she called it). This was why she sympathised with Ellen and did not condemn her.

'I saw Mrs Chase there tonight.' She knew of his interest in Maggie. 'Was Mrs Wylie there?'

'Didn't see her. No news of that poor boy. Ted Toller thinks he's dead.'

He took her hand. 'Goodnight, love.' Darling Dolly, so loving, so loyal, so safe.

Dolly went to bed, her mind a jumble of Sam, Maggie, Biddy and others, not meaning to disturb any of them by thinking about them, but disturbing herself.

Across the county in the delightful small town of Rotherford Royal, the man who was to be in charge of the new mental hospital planned for Lukesfield was giving a small dinner party to some close friends, doctors and their wives. He was an influential figure in their lives. He sat on all planning committees, knew his way through all administrative mazes, and could pull the purse strings better than most.

He was a good man, yet hard. He knew they called him the Executioner although he had never cut off any man's head. But he had hanged quite a few careers.

His closest friend, another bachelor, a Jungian-trained psychiatrist called Griff Williams, lifted his glass. 'A toast to your new post. Excellent claret, by the way.'

There was a rumble of conversation over dinner, during which the Executioner's voice could be heard saying, 'Once I'd had my attention drawn to it the site was exactly right.'

'You chose it?'

'A lot of people had a say in it, but in the end, yes, I think you could say it was my decision.'

'And you will be going?'

'I shall up sticks and go. I shall have to find a house.' A big house with a big garden was what he wanted. Although he was a bachelor he liked to spread himself. He collected books and large pictures, furniture to match. Also, the new job was a kind of promotion. What he wanted, anyway.

He held up a glass of wine to the light, through the gleam of red he saw the row of playwrights on his bookshelves. Shakespeare, Shaw, Coward, Sir James Barrie.

His eye rested on *What Every Woman Knows*. What was it Maggie had known? He had never been sure. That charm was a bloom on a woman? That woods were dangerous for walking in? He was not a great admirer of the little baronet, Beckett was more his man, so he did not continue with the thought, but just let it pass through his mind, unsolicited.

He was a medical man, a scientist, and although he admitted coincidence to his life, he did not go beyond. Even when, later, he heard the story of Lukesfield and came across, professionally, one of the chief characters in the drama, his only thought was how sad the case had not been picked up earlier when more help might have been given.

He was pragmatic, not a theorist. For his severely disturbed patients he never prescribed treatment without prolonged observation. 'Let's see 'em at it,' he would say.

But children do not like to be seen 'at it', and they develop their own ways of avoiding scrutiny. All of the parents in Lukesfield thought of themselves as loving, careful parents, nevertheless certain children wished to live their own private lives. There were different reasons. Later, much later, one of the Barbillon twins told his father that he had no idea how terrible it was always looking across the table at someone exactly like yourself, and *that* made them act the way they did. The Canadian boy, James, who cried so well, hated his sister. He never admitted it publicly but hate her he did, and he had reason. She had once tried to hang him. He was well on his way to hanging her when the Lukesfield saga blew up. These were specimen children; a couple of others just went along for the ride. Gangster material, probably. The children at the heart of it were disturbed children, the worst sort, the sort that did not show it.

This small group of children took its own way out. Physical escape is not easy when you are small and relatively weak. But children can do it through the mind, through imagination at play.

They were encouraged to use their imagination at Pettit's and this group did so. They were friends, but to be a group they had to have an initiation ceremony and these friends had one: each child had done something exceptionally wicked. One boy had pushed another into the pond and then run away; another had stolen his mother's purse to buy poison to kill his father; the girl had set fire to the house. Only the thief had been caught, none of the others, but *they* knew, they bonded to each other: they were a group.

A group has a ritual whether it acknowledges it or not. This group had a ritual. Since these were young children there was the minimum of ritual: the simple allegiance to a game. Do you believe in fairies?

Groups also always have a butt, a goat to sacrifice. It settles their boundaries, defines their character. This group had such a one. A non-person. An outsider.

They were all lost boys (except for Wendy) but he was more lost than most.

One they were teaching to fly, one they could shut in a drawer. To keep safe and dry, if it rained and was wet. One who did not answer back.

Next day it rained hard, was so wet in fact that the children did not come out to play, so it was a day for Maggie to search the Wendy House. *Was* it a good idea? Maggie asked herself, and had to admit that it probably was. Sooner done, sooner over.

She had had a bad night. Not full of bloody dreams, there never were 'bloody' dreams; if *she* saw blood then it was in full daylight. And take that for luck, she thought, but a restless, unsleeping night.

Her day (it was a Wednesday) was fully booked by Mrs James Teacher-Halliday, aged about ninety-nine, incorrigible hoarder of objects, some valuable, some worthless, all in need of a brush and wash, a prize gossip and great lady. Maggie enjoyed her Wednesday with Mrs Jimmy T.-H. (this was how she was known in Lukesfield). She enjoyed her housework, she loved the way in which steady physical labour cleared the mind and steadied the nerves.

The wet day had given Mrs Jimmy a cold, so she allowed Maggie to get on with her cleaning and depart, instead of trying to persuade her to stay on and drink tea and whisky as she usually did.

Maggie hurried on to Pettit's and the Wendy House. No one was around to look at her, although she could hear sounds of music from the main school building.

The atmosphere of the Wendy House knocked her back as soon as she got inside. It was pure, concentrated child. Cops and Robbers, Cowboys and Indians, children and adults, this was hostile territory where Wendy was queen.

But she knew at once that Sam was not hidden here.

No one could be unless they were flat, a shadow, fit to be shut in a drawer. And she knew where she had got that phrase from: the children had been chanting it. Nevertheless, it was rubbish. Whatever Sam was, he was also corporeal, a living, three-dimensional human being.

He could not be hidden in the Wendy House which was a toy with cupboards and shelves painted on the walls. A doll's bed stretched across one corner, and small wooden chairs and a table occupied the centre of the room. On the table was a miniature tea-pot and matching (if chipped) service of tea-cups and plates.

Maggie crouched (no room to stand upright – adults were carefully programmed out of this house), bending her knees to move around the room, investigating. She felt like a toy-town detective, a mini Sherlock Holmes. No, Miss Marples was more like it.

A couple of bright overalls such as the children always wore hung on a hook on the back of the door, a scuffed pair of plimsolls rested beneath them. The shoes were thick with dried mud.

Maggie took a look at the name printed inside: one was Mary Powell's. She noticed the shoes did not match, they were a rough pair. The other shoe was not quite the same style and was rather less muddy; it was unnamed.

Could she make that mean something? Not immediately. It didn't seem to say anything about Sam.

A bulge in the pocket of one yellow and brown overall caught her eye, she put her hand inside.

Leaves, more leaves, and a few twigs. Something more to be felt underneath, wrapped in a piece of cloth.

Maggie drew out a flat object with a pocket handkerchief folded around, more as a protection than a concealment, it seemed.

Holding it by the handkerchief she took a look. What she had was a cassette tape. There was a white label on the front on which a childish hand had written: 'The Lost Boy'.

Or it might be 'Boys' in the plural, the writing was not clear.

Maggie removed the handkerchief for a better look, taking the cassette tape in both her hands. Immediately a band of colour shot over her eyes.

Red waves rolled across her vision, blinding her with their brightness, then they passed away, and the customary zig-zag lights of a classic migraine attack followed them. Maggie crouched on the floor, waiting for the pain to begin.

No such thing. Her head remained clear as the dazzle faded and her vision became normal. She drew in a relieved sigh.

Then she looked down at her right hand which retained hold of the tape.

One of those curious visual blockages which can descend on the migraine sufferer appeared to have afflicted her. Her hand was blacked out and only the stump of her wrist was there.

A sickness rose in her stomach bringing with it, and as usual at such times, fear, dreading what she had to go through. No blood, though.

She felt her hand drop the cassette tape, it had to be done by an act of will, otherwise she might have held on till the harrowing of hell. The thought that she must drop the cassette, together with the will to do it, had struggled through her fear and come out on top.

The minute the missing fingers dropped the tape, her head cleared, with all pain, sickness and terror lifting, just as a migraine suddenly lifted, drawing aside like a curtain.

Maggie crouched where she was, drawing in deep breaths. Both her hands were with her and working normally. Only her heart seemed to have caught a disorder so that it was leaping and dancing in her chest, like a bird.

She crawled out of the Wendy House, leaving the tape and the handkerchief on the floor behind her. Then she went back in, wrapped the tape up in the handkerchief, being careful not to touch it, and put it into her pocket.

She had realised that, with her, touch or proximity to *something* triggered off her attacks.

The garden was still quiet and rain-swept as she made her way back to her car, the piano still going in the school. She was surprised that everything should be so normal.

She drove straight home, and rushed to put the tape on the player. She slotted it in, then stood there, listening.

Silence. Silence.

Then a high, breathing childish voice saying:

> 'Don't want to be useful. But I'll be good to the dead babies. I shall come out and sing gaily to them when the bell tolls; and then they won't be frightened. I shall dance by their little graves.'

and then:

> 'To die will be an awfully big adventure.'

Silence, once more.

Then the voice started again, repeating what she had just heard.

> 'I'll be good to the dead babies . . . '

and ending again:

> 'To die will be an awfully big adventure.'

Maggie turned the tape off. She had never heard Sam's voice, but she had no doubt it was he who was speaking.

If this was the 'speech' he had made at the Hallowe'en party no wonder the rest of the school had been powerfully affected.

The arrangement had been to ring Joe, but it wasn't him she wanted, she needed the warmth and strength of David.

He answered the telephone as quickly as if he had been sitting by it waiting for her call.

'Hello, I am glad it's you. I've been sitting here wondering whether to call you. I've got some news that I'm afraid is going to worry you. I've been wondering whether to tell you because it's confidential.' He was going to, however.

'I've got something to tell, too.'

'The word from Ted Toller is that his team believe the boy is dead, and they're going to take the mother in for questioning. She must know. More than she has said, anyway.'

'I don't think Sam is dead. Listen to me.' Quickly she described what she had found, and what had happened to her in the Wendy House. 'It's Sam's voice on the tape, I'm sure of it. And when I touched it, I had one of my "attacks". Call it stress migraine if you like, but I'm convinced they only happen when I am in touch with Sam. Literally in touch, somehow. Sound doesn't do it. When I *listened* to the tape I was fine, nothing happened. It must be some form of telepathy. I'm picking up nightmares *he* has. Or something like that. He must be interested in blood, he cut himself, remember? So he's alive, because I don't believe in supernatural things. He's alive all right.'

'Maggie,' began David, and she could tell from the way he said it that he didn't believe a word, and was about to be the voice of reason. 'If Ted Toller says the boy is dead that's good enough for me.'

Here was the parting of the ways between them, because although Maggie did not, could not, accept the overriding of certain natural laws, she did believe in the reality of unreason. Occasionally, without believing in supernature, you had to accept that odd things happened.

Maggie had to believe this, or she would be going mad.

'Listen to me,' David was saying. 'You've had these go's before, you've seen the doctor. You're just getting hyper-sensitive. Relax. Of course, anything to do with the boy starts you off. I can see that. But be reasonable. Hand on that tape. I don't say you should have taken it. You shouldn't. But since you've got it pass it on. The CID will have to have it.' Then he said: 'What's on it, anyway?'

'Quotations, I think,' said Maggie. 'From a dead author.'

'Oh that's marvellous – you make it so macabre. Maggie, steady up. And the quotes from beyond?' It was easy for him, he wasn't close to it, as she was.

'I'd be making a guess.'

'Make it.'

'Sir James Barrie: *Peter Pan*.' The Lost Boy's Tale: but she did not say that to David. The Little White Bird.

'I see.' He sounded baffled. 'Well, like I said. Get rid of it. Take it to the police.'

But Maggie shied away from that. 'Can't face them. Don't want them to know I've even touched it.'

'Give it to me then. I will give it to them.'

'And you'll tell them. They will ask and you will tell. You'll have to. No I'll post it.'

'Do it soon,' he ordered.

'See you,' she said dismally. It was not enough. She wanted help now. Joe Archibald *ought* to be on a telephone, she thought with anger. Leaving a message was not it, not enough.

All the same, she started to dial the number he had given her, but before she had finished her doorbell was ringing.

When she opened it she saw Joe himself. 'What's up?' he said at once. 'Something is.'

'How did you know?'

'I was at Pettit's trying to see Mrs Wylie again, and she let out she'd seen you running across the garden.'

'She saw me then?'

'You're not invisible.'

He was in the house, insistent, determined, in charge. They were in this together, he was her partner.

'That's it,' he said, when he had heard her story, and they had listened to the tape. 'They're into something, those kids. Some of them. Or one. Or all.' His voice trembled, went deep with emotion.

'Not all, surely?'

'No. But a group. What you've got there on that tape is a bit of ritual,' and, as Maggie made a demurring noise, 'not like going to church or crowning the Queen, but something they did together.'

'Is that how you see it?'

'Yes. I'm interested in psychology. I did a course once.' He had done courses in many things, had many lives. 'Kids do that. Certain kids, certain times.'

'Such as?'

'Well, when they are trying to create a world for themselves. Fantasy world, maybe, but real to them. It has to have rules, you see, bits of learned, regular behaviour, that's the key that turns the lock to open the door to let them in. Makes them a group.'

'And Sam?'

'He has to have a part in it, doesn't he? And we know who else – we both watched the Wendy House. We saw the children. Among others the brother Tom, and Mary Powell. They're the ones.'

'Do you think they've got Sam somewhere?' Maggie was hopeful.

'We can but look. You'll have to give this tape back or give it to the police.' He had been able to handle it freely, no trouble at all, but then this little bit of her story Maggie had edited out. David knew, he did not.

Some things one does not tell, thought Joe. As he had listened to the tape that anger he had known before rose in him so strongly that he almost screamed with rage. It was a pointed anger like a knife, and directed at Maggie. Thank God the tape was a short one, because the anger went when the voice stopped. But his headache was back.

Sam's voice had brought all that anger on.

'We've got to find Sam,' he said. What for? he asked himself. So I can feel *more* anger? What was the trouble with Sam that he came on like a disease? But then Sam had never been normal.

'He's alive,' said Maggie, replete as from an odious meal, with her own reasons for knowing it. 'The Lost Boy – it's the Barrie connection, isn't it?'

In 1904 there lived a small man with a head too large for his body, sad, hooded eyes set in a lined, moustached face. He had his boots hand-made in Piccadilly, knew where the finest guns and fishing-tackle in Europe were to be bought (and had bought them), but who had inside him a deep hole of misery that no worldly success could fill up. He knew that woods were dangerous places where you might meet the past and the future hand in hand. He knew that children die, and that other children, the lost ones, never truly know adult life. He was a man who knew how to make his misery work for him, make a myth of despair. In 1904 this man was writing a play about lost boys and one lost boy in particular which, at first, he called 'Peter and Wendy'.

Since he was a man of dark imagination this play for children had its sinister side. Barrie understood that children liked both to be frightened and to frighten. Death is an awfully big adventure, says Peter.

The small man had never heard of ecology, or pollution, or acid rain, but he knew instinctively that there is always a strange death in the air, and that some places, some growing things, some islands, woods and trees can pass on the miasma. Nor had he heard of Martha Littlebody, in 1904 she was buried and still forgotten, not yet resurrected by Arthur Chamberlain senior. But Barrie was a child of the Scottish Kirk to whom violence in religion was natural. Unlike the psychologist nicknamed the Executioner he did not believe in coincidences, but in destiny.

He was Miss Pettit's favourite author. Every year the school either acted a children's version of *Peter Pan* or were taken to see it. He exercised a powerful hold over her imagination (always had done since she screamed at Gerald du Maurier as Captain Hook when she was aged five), and through her it passed on to the children she taught. Some generations, tougher of mind, threw it off easily, others were possessed by it.

'Use your imagination,' she used to say to them. 'Open your mind to dreams, my darling. Imagine. Imagine.'

This was a man whose life had been shadowed by a dead brother. No one was ever going to blame Sir James Barrie for what went on in Lukesfield, but he certainly had a part to play. He was one of the bridges between minds; and in his brooding imagination he had always guessed he was just that.

'We can't look for Sam tonight. It's too late. And we've done enough for today.' (The shade of Sir James Barrie hung about, unconsciously exhausting her.) 'And tomorrow I will have to either put the tape back or give it to the police, perhaps both.'

'How both?'

'By putting it back and telling the police – we might see who had missed it and who came to look.'

'You're really turning this into your detective story.'

'No. Not so. I'm just being practical. We have to follow up what we have.' The decent thing to do would be to hand it over to Biddy Powell, but she knew she was not going to do that. To give it to Ellen, or even to tell Ellen, was best not thought of.

'What will you do?'

'Go there early tomorrow morning. Hang around. See what I can see. Then make up my mind.' She felt in charge, her mind cleared. Perhaps the haunts (she was beginning to call them the 'haunts', not migraine) had gone.

Joe considered. 'It seems to me you're right. You've got a head on your shoulders. I'll leave it to you. But you'll keep in touch?'

He too had steadied down, but in his case he remembered the anger and guessed it might come back. He would be better on his own when it did. Supposing he had hurt Maggie?

When Joe had gone she sat down to add up her account:

I am not sorry for Nicholas, although I started off full of sympathy. He has not given the support to Ellen which she needed; I am sorry for Ellen. Her instinct for self-preservation is strong, so that she took what action was necessary to keep her going as a person. Lovers, drink, the occasional outburst of anger, but she can be very silly. I am sorry for Sam.

The next day Maggie, bright-eyed and, on the whole, cheerful, telephoned Ellen to see if she was at home, and in reasonable shape. She was delighted to hear her cross voice reply. She had been sleeping, sleep must be a good sign. So with Ellen safely anchored, Maggie could get off on her own day's work. In an hour's time she had to collect Evadne, and Sophy and Elspeth, take them in her car to the outskirts of Lukesfield where a large and neglected villa awaited their services.

She had an hour in which to go to Pettit's School and replace the tape. Or else to watch if any child came to look for it.

If nothing worked within the hour then she could probably grab a space during the day to try again. If, at the end of the day, she had found out nothing then she would hand the tape to David, and thus to the police.

Who probably ought to have had it in the first place, anyway. Disloyalty to someone there had to be, but the person she could least afford to offer it to was Sam.

She went into the Wendy House, which looked untouched since she had been inside. If she put the tape back in the pocket of the school overall she could walk away and be outside it all.

Maggie disposed of it herself neatly behind a painted draught screen decorated with postcards.

When a child came to look in the pocket of the school overall it was Tom.

'Was this what you wanted?'

Maggie came from out of the screen, holding up the tape.

Tom was a beautiful child, without Sam's air of angelic innocence, but with a wide-eyed charm of his own. He had a splendid inheritance from each side of the family. Nothing wrong with his pool of genes.

'No.' He gave her a puzzled, blue-eyed stare. 'I came for my hanky. But it's gone.'

'Is this it?' Maggie held out the handkerchief which had been around the tape.

'No. Mine was a blue one. With spots.'

A lie if she'd ever heard one, but nothing to be done about it.

'Do you know what it is I showed you?'

'No.' He shook his head.

Another lie.

Supposing she said: It's a tape with your brother Sam's voice on it. Should she say it?

No, he was only a child, after all. She couldn't say it. She put the tape back in her pocket; later it could go to the police. She watched Tom run into school, not looking back at her.

But what could they have been doing with the tape? Who had made it and when? And what was the use of it? Apart from frightening others at the Hallowe'en party.

That Tom knew, she almost, but not quite, believed. He was Sam's brother, but Tom had the air of putting on an act, not his mother's son for nothing. She no longer knew what was truth and what was not.

As she had promised she left a prearranged message for Joe. He would know from it that a child had come to the Wendy House, but not which child. He'd get in touch with her. There was a built-in time-lag which worried her. Perhaps they should move faster.

The day passed, she worked with Evadne and Sophy and Elspeth. John Henry had gone on a week's tour with an Edward Bond play, rolling his eyes and saying he was more of a Pinter man but work was work. She missed John Henry, he livened things up with his sharp comments. Also he had a down-to-earth realism about the way he saw things that she could have done with now. Sophy had looked sad and peaky since John Henry went on tour. Something going on there no doubt. Small wonder. If John Henry had not been a full twenty years younger than she was herself, she could have taken him into her own bed. Might do yet. What a wicked thought. David would be furious, but it cheered her up. She began to have a dream of a different future from any she had envisaged.

She did some necessary food shopping on the way home, fish for her cat, chicken and salad stuff for herself, then turned towards her house.

Maggie was surprised to see her husband there. Outside was his old car which was even older than hers. He still had it, then. As she had hers still. Riches had not come to either of them.

'Can I come in?'

She stood aside. 'Of course. You've still got a key, haven't you?'

'Wouldn't use it. Lost my right to that freedom.'

They stared at each other, awkward, embarrassed. It was as if he had come back from the dead. Love, physical love, had gone, but a remembered affection remained and reawoke. He was nicer than she had remembered. But what did he want?

'Let's have a drink.'

He looked shabby, but quieter, and yes, it had to be said, happier, than when she had seen him last after their final quarrel. A bit thinner and soberer, too.

'Make it coffee. I'm off the other stuff.'

'Right.'

Over coffee he seemed to gather himself together to state his purpose.

'First, I've come to apologise for the way I cleared out. I'm ashamed of that.'

'Oh you made the odd phone call; I knew you were alive.'

'I deserve that.'

'I didn't mind at first, Chris, really. Then it began to hurt. Now I don't mind again. . . . But why did you?'

'I'd lost my job. I would never have been able to tell you.'

'Ah.'

'Yes. Nothing original about me.'

'And now?'

'I've come around, got another job, settled. In a way.'

'There's someone else?'

'Yes. That's why I'm here. I don't want to come back, Maggie. . . . And you don't want me back? No, I can see it. It's as well to be honest. The same reason as me? I'm glad of it.'

There was no other woman; he was simply trying to give Maggie her freedom. David had found him, called on him, and given him it straight: Let her go, let her out. But it was the right thing to do.

As he was leaving he said, with clumsy, belated fondness, 'You'll get in touch with me, Mags, if there's anything you ever want? Anything I can do?'

'Of course. Thanks.'

'We were never right here, you know. Not here in Lukesfield. It wasn't the place; we never fitted in. I don't like it, either.

Funny feel to the village. If you can call it a village. Bit too rich and fancy for my taste. We were happy till we came here. That's what went wrong with us, I think, this place. Did us in.'

'Is that how you see it?' Maggie could hear her voice rising with surprise.

'It's how I see it. So watch it. Don't let this place get you.'

Chapter Five

The day had not ended, although perhaps it should have done. Some days are better done with, over and gone.

Maggie had cooked supper, cleaned her own house, fed the cat, washed her hair and paid all outstanding bills. Everything that should have been done was done. Even her hair had gone as it should, falling into the correct curves around her face. She was consequently uneasy; it was unnatural for everything to be so orderly.

She found herself thinking about Chris. Not with regret – she was glad the past was parcelled up ready to be put away – but with surprise at what he had said. His analysis of why their marriage had failed was shrewd. The place was wrong for them.

So he had left Lukesfield, while she had stayed. That said something about both of them, although she was not sure what.

She went up and looked out of the window. A little summer mist hung over the trees. There was often a mist in Lukesfield, a light, white veil which wreathed the tops of the trees, without coming down to the roof-tops. Most of the houses in Lukesfield were low and sprawling, two storeys at the most. Many were bungalows. But they were all set in large, well-tended gardens. Not many flowers, since these did not do well in Lukesfield, but large shrubs and small trees. Even these needed much feeding since the soil was stony and poor, while the air was – the air was strange. Always damp, always heavy with different scents, some pleasant, some distinctly unpleasant.

As now. Perhaps other people did not notice, only Maggie Chase.

She sniffed: tonight the smell was of burning leaves. Well,

that was harmless enough. But one could never tell; she knew from experience that Lukesfield smells changed. Quickly too, sometimes. One minute you were smelling roses, and the next moment the charnel house seemed close. Nothing imaginative about that: it was the town tip, everyone knew that much.

Maggie closed the window. She would be selling the house and moving out herself when the divorce went through. Her and Ellen, that made something they had in common.

Somewhere under that damp sky was Sam, dead or alive. Was he sniffing at the air, enjoying the scent of burning? Or was he oblivious to everything, already being eaten away by little mouths.

Was it possible he had killed himself? The incident of the slashed throat came back to her with vivid clarity. Why had he done it? What was really the matter with him?

She had let David be altogether too reasonable here, explaining Sam's actions away as those of a disturbed child. Well, maybe. But maybe not. It ought to have been thought about more clearly.

She grubbed around in her mind for someone she could ask. Not David. She did not want the voice of practical good sense at this moment. What she needed was someone who *knew* about children like Sam.

There was no one to ask, but she was remembering something. She had read or heard something relevant. Television or radio? The radio, she remembered it now, one of those popular medical programmes. She could hear a distant quiet voice with a Scottish accent telling her that children who damaged themselves physically never hurt themselves significantly. Their self-abuse was a token only. A show, yes, real damage, no.

Sam's throat had been damaged all right. She'd dressed the cut and she knew. A little deeper and he'd have cut the jugular. But he'd drawn back.

So was it a token or something different? Did you have to believe that assured Scots voice? (Why did Scottish voices always sound so convincing?)

Then another voice intervened in this discussion that she was remembering, this voice, a woman's, suggesting that sometimes these children were very sensitive, ESP subjects.

Was it her own fault then, that because she had visions of blood Sam had cut himself?

The thought that there was a link between them was an alarming one. And yet it seemed to have been in her mind for a long time.

So long, in fact, that Maggie wondered if she had invented the memory of a broadcast talk in order to give it substance.

What about the Scottish voice then? It did sound very much like a man she had once known. Had he been the school dentist? And the woman's voice, now she came to think of it, was very like the elderly Miss Pettit's.

Out of the past the silent voices speak. If the dead do utter, they have to use someone else's voice, don't they? One cannot think (mediums apart) of the dead having voice boxes.

This thought flitted through Maggie's mind even while she guessed that on this occasion it was her own voice speaking.

Handling it with gloves, Maggie packed the tape in a stout envelope, and addressed it to the police. Then she walked through the dark streets to post it in the box. At last she was doing the right thing. What she did not know was that the police would sit on the news for two days, by which time it would be too late.

Joe telephoned when she came back from the post: she told him what she had done, she told him that Tom had looked for the tape, and had lied to her.

Joe said, 'I thought it would be the brother. Didn't you? Only one other possibility.'

Joe was her ally but he had little help to give her. She did not know what he meant.

'Pity he wouldn't talk. But he never would admit too much, that boy: his mother and father combined in him. And a touch of the Sams as well. Could talk, won't talk.'

'You realise what we've got to do? Where we've got to look?'

'In the woods? But the police have looked.'

The twigs and leaves in the pocket did point to the trees, always had.

'They didn't know where to look.'

'And do we?'

'I think so.'

'Tonight then? Now?'

'No, there is no moon. It would be too dark. But tomorrow early.'

As Maggie got into bed she thought the smell of a bonfire burning was stronger than ever. A penny for the Guy, she thought. But although we burn the Guy, Fawkes did not die by burning. He was racked, then drawn on a hurdle from the Tower to Parliament House, after which he was hung from the gallows, then drawn and quartered like a beast. Whether these barbarities were practised upon a body from which life had not yet flown is not clear. It is said that, on occasion, the executioner cut the body down while yet living, so that the full rigours could be inflicted on the living creature. This was known, among circles who were pleased to be jocular, as 'flaming the torch'.

Since it was winter and dawn came late, it was necessary to light flambards to complete the execution platform. The spectacle of death was to be public, with a large crowd expected. The crowds of the capital could become restless and wicked-natured if deprived of a good view. So the platform must be high, and yet not so high that the groundlings could not see. The enterprising landlord of the Westminster Tavern had erected a stand in which his customers could perch while supping their ale and mulled claret. It was customary to take hot drinks at a public execution so that the audience could better enjoy the warmth of their own living. Besides, if you did take a squeamish turn (some ladies did) then hot, spiced wine was a good reviver. The Westminster Tavern catered for the better sort of customer. This was a particularly fashionable execution, not because of the rank of the prisoner (she was a yeoman's daughter) but because of the nature of her crime. Attempted murder by poison of His Majesty, King James I. Some said the King himself would be present at Westminster to watch the protracted killing of Martha Littlebody. If so, he would be suitably masked. Others said No, His Majesty had no stomach for seeing blood spilt but would want the details afterwards. To which end he had sent a writer, Master George Webster, to put it all down. Master Webster's narrative was, later, much copied by many other hands, appeared in numerous broadsheets and penny-books, because of the truly sensational nature of the events that he witnessed. George Webster himself later committed suicide by taking hatter's acid, in which death he came near to reaching, but not surpassing, the agony of Martha herself. King James died in his bed, but his son perished upon a scaffold erected overnight like hers, and not far from the same place.

The knocking together of the planks for the scaffold did not reach to the Tower where Martha spent her last uneasy night. Not resting; you do not rest after the rack and other 'minor' tortures used to make you confess. Martha's shaky and faint signature on her confession testifies to the efficiency of the racking. Her co-conspirator, one of the King's cooks, and the French priest who had brought in the poison, and Henry Fitton, Martha's lover, suffered after her.

Martha came from a family of red-haired, white-faced women where the distaff side had kept secretly to the old religion. They were women of great height, strong passions and flaming tempers, whose husbands died young. Henry Fitton came from a long established family of recusants; he had been hidden by Martha Littlebody in a den on her father's Kentish farm. Henry was a courier between England and a group based in the Low Countries who planned to kill King James.

Martha Littlebody was arrested in London, in the royal kitchens with the cook. She was eighteen; a short life and a public death.

She did not give in easily, even the executioner was surprised at the oaths that rolled from Martha's lips as she was racked. A screaming, raging voice shouted out her agony, full of anger, an anger that would not be appeased.

She raged, she was obscene, they knew it, but could not blame her, only turn the screws tighter. Hearing her, it was hard to believe she could have wished to kill the King out of Christian love, there must have been a fury at the bottom of it all. She was a fury. Her mission came from the Devil, there could be no doubt about it.

She was not a witch. King James made particular enquiries as to this, being anxious as to possible after-effects. But he was assured that, even on torture, she had given no signs, and of a possession migrating through the generations, the little Scot had no idea.

Anger can be buried, sleep, and reawaken, moving through other people's minds and bodies. Anger can go vegetable and grow like a tree.

Before it was fully light the audience had begun to gather. The street traders selling sweetmeats and fairings came first, seeking out good pitches to sell their goods. They had smelt out the feel of the day beforehand, and knew that trade would be lively. After the pedlars with their kickshaws came the tricksters selling cures against the pox, for impotence, for sterility; potions to create love, to kill love, powders for long life, in men, dogs and horses.

A small crowd watched the cart trundle out of the Tower, then proceed at a fair pace through the streets to Parliament House. Martha's conveyance came first, then that of her three companions in misery. She was granted the courtesy of being the first and being alone. But you are never alone with pain. A larger crowd greeted the arrival of the small procession. A coach deposited a clutch of richly cloaked and furred dignitaries. Men of position, whose presence the King and the law demanded. Nearby stood grooms with their horses, their masters in a flamboyant bunch, drinking mulled wine. Seated not far away a group of court ladies prattling in French.

The crowd grew bigger as the hour for the hanging of the woman approached. The cart had come to a rest. The occupant inside had felt the thump of the wheels grinding over the cobbles. The timbers of the cart creaked like a straining ship, or the branches of an old tree in the wind. She could hear the voices of the crowd outside, might have stood there herself if the political situation in England had been reversed, she was not a sensitive woman. People said that Martha was now paralysed on the right side as a result of her racking. This was not entirely true, she could move, but with fierce pain. The distortion was great: one hip had shifted its position so that her pelvis was twisted.

Through her pain she could hear the voices outside: she was very angry, her pain became anger and her anger was pain, impossible to distinguish between the two, they fed on each other.

Master George Webster's account of what followed was repeated, glossed, exaggerated, forgotten, finally to surface in Lukesfield in the twentieth century.

Martha was dragged out to the gallows on her hurdle. The sight of the tall, large-boned, well-fleshed figure with her red hair tied back behind her ears produced a sudden hush, followed by shouts and calls, all hostile. The court ladies were silent, then murmured to each other in low voices, closet talk.

Martha was dressed in a stained shift of natural linen, all her own clothes (she had been finely dressed when arrested, her father was not poor) had long since disappeared. Also her jewellery. She had had an amethyst ring that she valued greatly; that was gone. She had once worn a silver comb in her hair; gone also. Her father had sent in a bag of silver, gone also, and into the right hands.

Nevertheless:

'How will it go then?' The assistant to the Public Executioner to his Majesty, come up for the day from his small Surrey freeholding, spoke to his master.

A kind of grudging mutter was the answer. But it was interpreted and understood.

'Ah, now that I thought would not be the case here. A woman, and there having been an easement to our pockets.'

The Executioner spoke in his deep, decided bass: 'The word has come down from above.' He stumped forward. 'So I flame the torch.'

Martha Littlebody was hoisted into position, the noose placed about her neck. As her body rose, to dangle, feet swinging, the crowd went quiet again.

Death by hanging is a messy business, but the stream that descended from between Martha's legs was bright red. And then a small bundle appeared to hang at her feet like a puppet.

A hush descended on the crowd before the noise rose again louder than ever.

Perhaps they were shocked for all their practicality about necessary death. Master George Webster was shocked and would have crossed himself (for he too had hankerings after the old religion) if the place had not been so public.

Martha Littlebody had not pleaded that she was enceinte. *Had she done so her execution would have been postponed. She had preferred to take the child with her.*

Mother and child were cut down from the scaffold. Martha was certainly not quite dead, for she moved one hand. Her body was tied to four horses, opened up with a sword, and drawn apart, a job roughly done because the horses took fright. It was then that one hand became separated from the rest and fell among the crowd. Where it went after that, Master Webster does not record.

Later, the remains of Martha and her child were carried to Kent by her father and secretly buried in an area of woodland on his farm.

A tree was planted above to mark the spot.

Maggie and Joe reckoned without the weather which prevented their searching for Sam. A night of heavy rain was followed by two days of thick, white mist which made even crossing the road dangerous. The police search too was hindered, and if they had the tape they were saying nothing.

Maggie woke in the thick night, just before dawn on the third morning. She moved restlessly; she felt a warm stream of blood issue between her legs. Well, it was to be expected at this time of the month. She got up to deal with it. She had no fear of real blood, only imaginary blood.

As soon as it was light she got up and dressed. Today was the day when Sam must be found. She knew now where Joe had his living quarters so she would go there to get him out. It had been more or less settled between them yesterday. She would just be hurrying it up a bit.

Chief Superintendent Ted Toller awoke early also on that morning as was his habit. He looked across to his wife sleeping in the other bed; she looked flushed, and happy. A good dream going on there, obviously. His own had been rather unpleasant, but he could hardly remember the details now except that he had not enjoyed it. He was an imaginative man who had a varied selection of nasties (collected on the job) pushed to the back of the mental cupboard. Memory had extracted a morsel from there, no doubt, to furnish his nightmare.

He went into the kitchen to make a cup of tea. He sat there sipping it.

His wife appeared, still pink and happy. She poured herself a mug of tea. She was younger than her husband, of the mug generation.

'You're worried.'

He grunted.

'It's about the boy.' It wasn't a question from her, it was a statement.

'You're thinking he's dead?'

'I know it.'

'He didn't run away then? That's the story going round, that she beat him and he took off. Childish games and all that. They say.'

'I don't know where you get these tales from.'

'Well, not from you. You never say a word.'

He looked at her. He told her everything, and she knew it. But they kept up a public fiction that he was discretion itself.

'He's dead, love. He's got to be.'

There was a kind of exasperated misery in his voice. His wife studied him.

'Yes? Well, I know you. You don't pluck that out of the air. You're not inventive. You have a solid fact to go on. Not just feeling.'

'It is a feeling; a strong feeling, the mother's story is so full of holes.' Then he said with a rush, 'I broke Mrs Powell yesterday. She told me what she didn't want to tell; the kid had bruises on him. More than once. Yes – all right so we'd heard the tale about it before. But that was gossip. This was a woman who had *seen* for herself. Bruised like a lizard.'

'Like a lizard.'

'That was what she said: she meant he was mottled with bruises.'

'Is that all?'

'I think it's enough. Not proof, but enough for me. His mother overdid the beating and killed him.'

His wife thought about it. She knew her husband very well.

'There must be a little something *more*.'

'The mother drinks and has a lover.'

'So does half of Lukesfield. That's not it.'

He always trusted her, so he told her about the tape which had arrived anonymously two days ago.

'I've held back on doing anything, thinking about it even, till I could be convinced it was genuine. Even now I'm not sure. They've done what tests they can and for what it's worth tell me it really is a boy's voice of about the right age. It worries me.'

Ted Toller was not, and never could be, a channel of communication in this business; he was a solid man, contained in his own body, completely of himself. This was his nature.

Maggie's nature was to have a loving sympathy, drawing out thoughts like sucking poison from a wound.

This time she had caught Joe's mood. When she arrived he was up, dressed and drinking the acorn-coffee he preferred as being less destructive to the environment than ordinary coffee. Pigs and pannage, he said, and to Maggie's raised eyebrows, 'That's what you'll find in the Domesday Book for St Lukes Field. Pannage for so many pigs. Universal food, acorns were.'

'Do you pick your acorns in Lukesfield?' He was a man of strangely gathered bits of knowledge, she thought.

'No, buy them ready washed in tins, Come on, let's go search for the boy. . . . Come along, Maggie-larger-than-life.'

'Is that what you call me?' They were getting into her car.

'To me you are. You capture the imagination.'

Maggie started the car, and drove off. And you capture mine, she thought. That is, you interest me. I wonder about you and don't seem to come to any understanding.

She drove back into the heart of Lukesfield. On top of the dashboard in front of her were spread out the leaves found in Tom's pocket with the tape of Sam's voice.

Joe had identified the leaves as ash, and an oak.

So they were going to look for a clump of trees made of oak and ash, standing close together.

There might be many such, or none at all. They didn't know, they were playing guesses.

Tendrils of the late fog, just dispersing, still lay over the tops of the trees, looping down and around in ethereal, moving rings. It was pretty, romantic and yet sombre too. In theory this woodland was an attractive place, in practice nothing made it likeable.

They started off on their task.

Just as they got going, Ted Toller was on the telephone sending out the order for that same area to be searched again. He was talking down all those who might have had other ideas (such as *not* searching it again), pulling his rank, ordering it done, now, this minute. Behind it was an early telephone call from the police laboratory dealing with the tape of Sam's voice. When the tape had been played again, with its sounds intensified, you could hear birds singing. You could also hear the sound of a train. Ted Toller listened to the sound of the train, heard the birdsong and then consulted a large map on which virtually every tree of importance was marked.

Trains and birds spelt out the same message to him that the leaves had to Joe, the nature lover.

There were other trains, other trees, other birds, but this site carried conviction to Ted Toller. He was several hours behind Joe and Maggie. Thus the police team set out on their search just as Joe and Maggie were ending theirs.

They had entered the wood hand in hand, clinging together like children, not talking much, but moving around quietly. On her way over Maggie had considered calling on Ellen to tell her what she and Joe were about to do, she had said it seemed only fair, but Joe had said No, Ellen was not to be dragged in. It was going to be bad enough for her, anyway, leave her out of this. He seemed to see more into the future than Maggie could herself at the moment, although she had a presentiment that whatever they found it was not going to be very good for Ellen.

Elm, ash, oak. Oak, ash, and elm. There were plenty of trees in the right relationship to each other, all young and scrawny, none healthy-looking, but it was interesting that elm was making a come-back. Perhaps the acid rain had killed off the virus. Or a natural immunity had come about.

They had dropped hands but stayed close together.

They were better searchers than the police in that their technique was more efficiently adapted to what they were seeking. The police had kept their eyes on the ground; Maggie and Joe looked upward, treewards all the time.

They stopped before the big oak, the biggest tree in the wood, the one that flourished. An elm and an ash tree were its neighbours. Or near enough.

Joe looked at the trunk of the tree, and then stared upward through the branches.

'I think we're here. Yes— Clever. A neat job.'

Maggie too studied the tree trunk. She touched a little heel of wood where a branch had once been. There was another such just above, and another beyond that. Nimble legs and hands could scramble up.

'Why didn't the police see?' Maggie wondered.

'Were they looking? Not for this. Not for what you and I see.'

'No. . . . ' She considered. 'Can you get up? Or shall I?'

'Both of us. One after the other. That's how it's done. You first and I'll come behind.'

'Will it bear my weight? Yes, I suppose so.'

Maggie scrambled up the tree, finding the foothold surprisingly secure, and grabbing branches for extra support. As soon as her head was up among the leaves, she looked around, feeling more like a character out of *Alice in Wonderland* than Sir James Barrie.

To her right she could see a wooden platform, well disguised with leaves and branches, all fresh, none withered, so that they must be constantly renewed; done cleverly, with leaves taken from neighbouring trees so that the oak would not miss them. A curtain of leaves protected the platform from her full view. It was a tree-house; a children's playing place. She had had one herself as a child, but nothing like as good as this.

Silently she scrambled along to it; Joe following. He seemed to know where he was going better than she did.

When reached the platform was surprisingly secret, surprisingly secure, like a green cave.

But it was empty. Sam was not here.

They looked at each other with disappointed eyes.

'He's been here, swear,' said Joe, looking at the scatter of leaves, ash and elm as well as oak on the floor of the tree-house. 'You know it's quite livable in, if you are a little boy not quite sure who and what you are, anyway. . . . He's been tearing up leaves. Look – ' He pointed to small deposits of shredded leaves, now shrivelled and dried.

Maggie had a sudden picture of a bored, idle Sam picking at the scabs on his throat, then turning to the leaves, each activity as casual and aimless as the other. Sam had been here, but was here no more.

They stayed a little while, studying the tree-house, which was ingeniously clever in its construction. Solid lengths of branches lashed together to form a floor. They saw that plaited raffia and sacking made the base for the curtain of leaves and small branches which were slotted into neat little pockets. The whole apparatus looked old, as if it had been made over generations of children, but brought up-to-date by new hands.

Maggie thought about that: it made interesting thinking, a secret, child hide-away, the knowledge passed down the generations. Or did successive children rediscover it by accident? Either way, there was a kind of magic at work.

They slid to the ground, Maggie first, then Joe. On the ground they faced each other.

'He's been there. And not so long ago either. What else was in the pocket?'

'Pebbles.'

No more words passed between them, Joe led the way, and Maggie followed.

Beyond the trees was a more open patch of land, covered with scratchy tags of wild roses, big with thorns, clumps of bristling thistles, and rank nettles. A small pond gleamed with an evil eye in the morning sun. In the middle of the pond like the pupil of that eye was the tiny island, pebbly and rough.

The island that would not disappear, the island.

Even from where they stood they could see the curved form of a child, lying with head extended and arms stretched, feet neatly pointed, as if flying.

The notion of flying was important. Children often think they can fly. Perhaps some children can flutter a few inches before flopping to the ground. But there are some drugs that give you hallucinations, make you think you are free as a bird. Marihuana does. Ellen had marihuana. You could smell it sometimes. Had she given it to Sam to quieten him? Or had he stolen some because he liked it? Supposing he sat in the tree smoking, and then flew?

In the distance, beyond the trees, the two of them, hand in hand again, heard the police arriving.

The last little boy that Joe had seen dead, unmistakably, manifestly dead, as opposed to the boy seen slumped in the front seat of a crashed car who might have survived, or the lad seen thrown from his horse who might *not* have broken his neck, that boy had been his only brother.

They were twins, Joe and Edward, known as Teddy, identical twins, nourished by the same placenta. One day their mother went out leaving them in the charge of their elder sister. (They had no father, as far as Joe was concerned they never had had a father). Relations between the brothers and their sister were friendly but detached. She did not notice when the two boys took their cycles and rode off out of the house. She was reading a book. Not a comic, a book; to read a book was virtuous, her mother had said.

The two boys pedalled off to a building site where a number of trees were being cut down to make way for a block of flats and a new school.

The trees were beautiful, and in full leaf with the scent of summer on them. Joe always remembered the smell of those green and living leaves.

A lorry piled high with the cut-up tree trunks, with several branches heaped on top, was just backing out of the building site when it was hit by a car travelling too fast along the main road. The lorry shuddered to a halt and its burden, which must have been badly loaded, toppled over and showered down upon Teddy, who was staring up at them.

Joe never forgot the sight of his brother, spreadeagled on the ground before him, with leaves and branches over and around him. A tree trunk had smashed his head in. Bruises spread all over Teddy's body as Joe watched; it was an extraordinary sight. Blood appearing spontaneously before his very eyes.

But the most extraordinary thing was that what Joe grieved for was not his brother, but the trees, living beautiful trees so freely destroyed. He did not cry for Teddy, but for the trees.

The police arrived as Maggie and Joe stood by the body of Sam. Maggie saw them through the trees and waved them to come on. With their arrival Maggie knew her part was over for the time being.

She looked down at the body of Sam, wondering how long he

had been dead, and thinking how strangely neat and clean he looked, almost as if he had been washed.

The two of them, Joe and Maggie, were pushed aside by the police. At first ignored, then given a brisk, first questioning. There would be more to follow, that was implied, but for now it was over. Then they were free to leave.

A crowd had already gathered in the road outside; Maggie and Joe threaded their way through it. Maggie noticed a hostile attitude towards them, faint but detectable. They were infected people, they had been close to something terrible, and no one wanted to be near them.

'Come back to breakfast.'

Joe grunted. 'Nothing much. Couldn't eat. Just a drink.'

Over a mug of hot tea, he said, 'What did you make of that place?'

'Nasty,' said Maggie, suddenly and spontaneously, surprising herself with the force of her reaction. 'Worse than I thought.'

'It was, wasn't it? But I've never liked that piece of land. . . . That tree-house was old, you know. Been there years. Patched up, of course, and made-do. Wonder how many kids knew about it? As many as wanted to, I suppose. Ever heard talk of it? Maggie shook her head silently. 'Did you notice anything about the boy?'

'His face was bruised. And his arms. He looked as though he had been beaten.' Beaten to death? No, she could not bear to ask what that might mean.

'Yes, he was bruised. I saw that. Don't know what to make of it. Notice anything else?'

'He was too clean.'

'So you did see. Yes, he'd been washed. All over I think.' He stared into his mug of tea. No answer there.

The thought of Sam being washed did not make either of them feel any better.

To her surprise Maggie found she was praying. She was saying: Make it good for Sam. Wherever he is make it good for him now. We are in circles, Sam and I. I do not know how a channel was opened up, but I sense it was. Save me with him. There *is* something to save me from, I know it.

As she spoke, inside herself a thin veil of red crept round the corner of her eyes; she almost saw it but not quite. She shook her head to shake the red mist away. She made a huge effort at repulsion. To her great relief it rolled back, her eyes were clear and she could see the sun shining brightly.

While all this was going on, Joe must have said goodbye and left.

From evidence later received obviously she spoke to him and said goodbye back.

Police activity set Ellen, Nicholas, Maggie and Joe on little islands on which they could only be reached by their friends with difficulty. They were hedged about with prohibitions of fear. People wanted to get in touch with them but they were frightened. Or physically impeded by the fact that there was a policeman in the house, as there all too frequently was.

This apart, everyday life went on. Maggie cleaned houses with her High-Lo team, Joe went to work, and Nicholas kept in touch with his office. Ellen drank. Or so everyone presumed, since the brief glimpses of her hurrying from the house to a waiting police car, and then from the police car to the house made her look as though she did.

Maggie telephoned Ellen as soon as she could on the day after finding Sam, a Wednesday, but Ellen would not talk much on the telephone. Nor did she wish to receive visitors: she would grieve on her own.

'You ought not to be on your own. Are you on your own?'

'Nick certainly isn't here.' Ellen gave a hoot of melancholy, wine-laden laughter.

'What about what's-his-name?' Your lover, she meant.

'You don't think he's been around, do you? Hates me now. Thinks me guilty. You don't know how ruthless . . .' muttered Ellen.

Another bloody male running for cover, translated Maggie. Nicholas was the same. The story was that since Sam's disappearance he and Biddy had quarrelled badly. The men in Maggie's own life now were doing their best to help her. David, and also Joe, the new quiet, chastened Joe, were with her as much as they could manage. ('You promised,' Joe said, 'the morning we found the boy. I said would I be welcome and you said Yes.') David knew about Joe now, but was managing not to be jealous. Just.

Maggie could have been happy if she had not been so desperately worried and perplexed. Sam, it all came back to Sam, what had happened to him, touched her. Circles were interlinked.

'Goodbye, Ellen, I'll keep in touch.' She became aware that Ellen had already put down the telephone so she was keeping in touch with nothing. Was it her imagination, or had she heard Ellen breathe softly over the line, 'My position is much worse than you think. You don't know how bad it is with me.'

On that same Wednesday, the day after Sam's body had been found, Maggie and Evadne had an arrangement to clean a house in Barleyhill Drive. Barleyhill Drive was the smartest and most expensive road in Lukesfield. It was a pleasure to clean Barleyhill Drive, Evadne said, made you feel gold dust could rub off all over you.

They parked the car, and as they did so, another car drove up behind them.

'Nicholas.' Evadne looked frightened. 'I knew he was looking for you. He wants to ask something. He telephoned me to find out where we'd be. You weren't answering.'

'I know.' After six obscene telephone calls and three accusations of 'knowing more than she said,' Maggie was not answering her telephone. She could guess what Nicholas wanted to ask about.

She walked round her old Volvo to Nick's smart BMW, not so well polished these days as once, but still a symbol of prosperity and advancement. The same was true of Nicholas himself, not so well polished, but still the rising young executive. He came to the point at once.

'You found Sam, you saw him, you got a good look?' It was hardly a question, the question was coming. 'You saw the bruises?' Maggie hesitated to answer. 'Go on, you did. Tell me what you saw. Remember I've seen him too, I identified him, Ellen didn't.'

'I saw bruises on his face and arms. Side of his face. Legs, too. Yes, bad bruises.'

'Ellen wouldn't look at him. Cried. Do you think she killed him?'

'I can't answer that.'

'Sam was beaten to death. The police don't admit that yet, waiting for the post-mortem, but I know.'

Evadne appeared round the side of the BMW. She was listening.

'You could be wrong,' said Maggie. 'Why don't you wait and see?'

She wasn't an expert on death by violence, but there were one or two things that made her wonder exactly how and why Sam had died.

The washing for one thing.

Nick was not done with her. 'The police played me a tape. They wanted me to say if it was Sam's voice. I don't know if it was Sam. I've hardly heard him speak. Biddy says it could have been. He made a great spiel about death or something at that Hallowe'en party. We've disagreed about it,' said Nicholas grimly. 'She can be bloody obstinate, that woman.'

'Is that all?'

'No, it's not. I've been questioning Tom. The police got the tapes anonymously through the post. Tom says he saw you putting them in a pocket of his overall. And that when you saw him you ran away.'

'That's a lie.' But it had a bit of truth in it. Enough to stick, which was clever of Tom. 'I was taking it out.'

'You mean Tom had it? I don't believe you. Have you told the police?' he challenged.

'I've told one policeman.' David. Thank God she had told David.

'I'm going to tell them what Tom said. I don't understand the tape or what it means. But it was part of Sam's death scene. And you seem part of that, Maggie. You found my child, you had that tape. Perhaps you made it.'

I am an ordinary person to whom extraordinary things are happening, Maggie had told herself. What was happening now was an extension of this: out of nightmare into everyday life, which might itself join in the nightmare and become hideous.

'I don't know anything about the death of Sam. Or the tape,' she told his father. But all the same it was not true. In some way she was intimately connected.

Was it this that had hung at the back of her mind with a curtain of foreboding? A pre-knowledge that she was to be accused of Sam's death.

For a moment there was a red prickle of dots before her eyes like tiny pin-points of blood, but they faded even before she had time to take them in. Then a blackness dangled before her eyes, creating a specialised form of tunnel vision round which she could see, but whose centre was impenetrable. Yet the centre swung: movement was perceptible. A tiny swinging body, miniaturised but solid.

Out of the dark shadow crept a fantasy that she had not known lived in her mind, which was that she had hanged herself, hanged herself, but hung there still alive.

And as if that was not an unpleasant enough thought, she had the distinct impression that something even worse lay behind it. An idea that she might always live in that dark shadow, never to come outside in the sunlight again. It was not dreams of blood she had to fear, those might or might not be the aura of migraine, but darkness itself.

Her terrors which had seemed linked with Sam had not ended with his death.

Nicholas said, 'Are you all right? You've gone very white. I didn't mean to frighten you.'

He was right outside her nightmare, would never be in it, and, for a moment, she hated him for that freedom.

Ted Toller had before him the police pathologist's report on Sam's body, so he knew more about the way Sam had died than either his parents or Maggie and Joe.

He was as interested in the bruising as the others; his eye flicked over what the pathologist had to say. The report said the obvious things about age and weight, noted the signs of an 'earlier injury to the throat', and went on to comment on the bruising.

'As a general rule the greater the force, the more extensive the bruise . . . the body was extensively bruised. There were bruises on the trunk, arms, legs and buttocks.

'These bruises were of two sorts; those on the arms and legs were rounder, and were probably caused by a hand or a fist. I would judge them to be one to two weeks old.'

Ted Toller said aloud, 'Done before he went missing then. I knew his mother beat him up.'

But had she killed him?

'The second category of bruises are new, and occurred from injuries shortly before death, and are associated with fractures of the limbs, ankles, and wrists. There was a comminuted fracture of the base of the skull, together with contre-coup lacerations.

'These injuries are consistent with a fall from a standing position.'

Ted Toller let out a whistle. This wasn't reading the way he had expected. He got up, walked to the window and looked out. His room had a window opening on to an inner courtyard where a solitary cat sat sunning itself while savouring the smells from the canteen kitchen across the yard. The smells of Irish stew and fried fish reached Ted simultaneously, but his nose was able to sort them out at once.

Which was more than he could do with what he was reading now. What did it all mean? A fall. From where?

He felt depressed. He had believed that he knew what had happened to Sam; his mother had killed him by accident, lost her head, and tried to hide his body. Now it all looked different.

'These injuries would have caused unconsciousness but were not the cause of death.'

Ted Toller took a deep breath. Now it was coming.

'The blood is very dark, and fluid. The right auricle and ventricle of the heart are distended with blood . . . the large veins are full of blood, the brain is deeply engorged. Small subendothelial ecchymoses are found on the serous surface of lungs and heart.

'Traces of grass, leaves, and pollen are to be found in the nostrils, mouth, throat and ears. There are marks of violence about the mouth and throat. . . .

'Death was by asphyxiation, probably by leaves and vegetable matter being pressed down upon the face. The subject would already have been unconscious.'

Ted remembered that his wife wanted him to bring back a bottle of dry sherry and some aspirin when he came home that evening: they were entertaining some friends to dinner. He drew the telephone towards him. It was unlikely he would be home in time.

He understood what medical details about the blood meant: it was the body struggling to live when the mind had given up.

Ellen would shortly be taken down to the police station for a day-long session, and her neighbours would be questioned about her way of life, and what they knew of it in detail. He would get nothing from this and some premonition told him so. Or was it just that as an experienced policeman he knew already that Ellen was a talker but not a teller. She was an actress, you had to remember that, she could cover up what she wanted to cover and let you see only what she wished.

He had no children himself and therefore was the more troubled by the death of a child.

The last item on the pathologist's report troubled him most of all.

'The body has been cleaned up. Not thoroughly washed, but adequately. The cleaning agent, of which traces remain, was a scouring powder, probably a proprietary brand called Flight.'

Flight was tinted a pale green while its competitors were either white or blue in colour, thus it was easy to identify. There was also the smell which was pine, but Sam had been dead long enough for this not to count. You did not smell pine, you smelt Sam.

Why had Sam been washed?

Smothering, like hanging, is, in some respects, a messy death. In dying the body rids itself of its rubbish.

Thus Ted Toller, raising those brush-like eyebrows which his wife longed to cut, could decipher the washing. But why do it?

There was an answer, and that answer was Ellen. A mother might wash her child clean.

But use Flight, which was an abrasive powder with bleach in

it? Was that a motherly act?

His telephone rang before he could dial his own call. 'Sherry,' said his wife. 'Remember? And home early, remember that too?' Also aspirin, but of that he had a permanent supply in the bottom left-hand drawer of his desk.

Not bothering to answer her, he said, 'Have you got any Flight in the house? It's a cleaner.'

'I know what Flight is. We've all got some, I should think. There was a drum on every doorstep as a promotion gift. We all have it, and most of us use it.'

So Ellen, Maggie, Biddy at Pettit's School, old Miss Pettit herself, Joe Archibald, everyone who had known Sam and many who had not, had supplies of the cleaner.

Teams of detectives could have gone round Lukesfield enquiring about the sales of Flight and the investigation would have been useless.

He did not tell his wife of what lay behind his query, but she guessed, and because she was angry that he would not be home early, might not be home at all, she dropped her usual rule of absolute discretion, and talked to her best friend Annabel.

By the end of that day everyone in Lukesfield who wanted to know about it knew two things: that Ellen Wylie had been questioned all day at the police station and then returned to Oakwood, and that she had beaten her son to death, buried him, then dug him up and washed him.

The details, true or untrue, did not matter. But there was enough truth in them to damn Ellen.

That night Ellen, a little the worse for drink, heard something putter through her letter-box. It was a little bundle of excrement, human or dog, it was not clear which.

Ellen did not clean it up; she gave it a look and left it there. Two drinks later she heard another noise. More distant and quieter. Drunk she was, but not deaf.

It was the sound of the garden gate being closed. Then laughter.

Avoiding the nastiness at her front door Ellen went out by the side door to investigate.

At her gate some hands had deposited a dead dog. A very dead dog. Judging by its appearance, it was a dog that had been buried and then dug up.

Ellen did not touch this either. Instead she went inside and telephoned Maggie.

'Tell the police. Let them deal with it.'

As a result all the next day a lonely policeman passed Ellen's gate at intervals as a protection. He was not there all the time, the police have many jobs. Looking after Ellen was only one.

But Ellen, under siege, knew now she was hated. She had lost her husband and both sons. She had just enough to drink, giving herself a kind of drip-feed over the next few days, to deaden the pain but not to wipe it out. The police questioned her again, several times, but so far had not arrested her. She reckoned she was a few days off from that yet. She gave herself about forty-eight hours.

There was a way into Oakwood through the belt of trees behind the gravel-pit land, then by a hole in the fence into the Wylies' garden. She was surprised when a tap on the garden door made her realise she had a visitor.

'Who is it? she said cautiously, behind a chained door.

'Come on, you know.'

'You have to say.' Ellen struck an obstinate note.

'You can *see*, damn it.'

Ellen started to shut the door.

'Charley Soul,' he said hastily.

'Enter, Charley Soul. Aren't you afraid the police will see you visiting me? That's a position of high danger.'

'I took care.' He came inside. 'Besides, they kind of gave me permission.'

'What's that?'

'One day I'll explain.'

They went into the kitchen and sat down at the table. Ellen advanced to the refrigerator to get out a bottle of wine. She liked her wine white, dry, and cold, all the things she felt she wasn't herself. The disarray in the kitchen was considerable, and Charley Soul took it in.

'You shouldn't stay here. This house is no good for you.'

'Nowhere else to go.'

'I think you have.'

'I give myself about forty-eight hours,' said Ellen.

She opened the refrigerator door whereupon a large, blood-stained parcel fell to the floor. There was yet another pushing behind it. Ellen took no notice, just kicking it aside with her foot, and reaching inside for her bottle.

After a pause, Charley Soul said, 'What's that?'

'Just one of Nick's parcels of venison.' Ellen was indifferent. 'They keep arriving. One bloody bundle after another. . . . Joke.'

'Don't they. . . . ' he hesitated, 'smell a bit strong?'

'So-so.'

'Can't you do something about it?'

'I did think of burying them, but I don't fancy being caught burying bundles of flesh. I might get lynched.'

A glass of wine for each was laid on the kitchen table.

Charley said, 'I'll help you bury them. You come with me and I'll help you.'

'Oh Charley is my darling,' said Ellen, swigging her wine in a great gulp. 'Why bother?' She pushed his glass towards him. 'Drink up since you are here.' She watched him take a sip. 'Not poisoned, you know. So, do you wish me well?'

'For God's sake, what's got into you? Do you doubt it?'

Ellen shrugged. 'I don't know why you are here. I thought you'd be out spreading God's word on the world. I thought you'd dropped me; I don't blame you. Mind you, I didn't like you for it, either.'

Now she laughed, and put her hand upon his lips. It was not that she thought he loved her, she knew he did not, but she was convinced that she held a magic for him that kept him in thrall.

Her hand held to his lips was like a kiss. He told himself that Lucifer's kiss before that Fall must have been much like this, full of love but rich with future sin. Ellen being a woman was the only difference, arch-angels being, as far as he knew, not sexless but men and women both. That was his heresy. Also that the Fall was not something dead and past but something that everyone had to go through. Ellen was approaching hers now.

'Do you believe in evil?'

'I believe in bad luck,' said Ellen, with conviction.

'Unluck moves forward in time. Evil stays still for ever.'

'What *are* you talking about?'

'I will move forward with you.'

'What *are* you saying?'

Charley Soul was suddenly practical. 'Bring the meat. I'll show you where to bury it. And pack a case. You need never come back here. You can't stay in any case.'

'Why not?'

'That ill luck you were talking about. You're not popular here. Better out of it. I'll take you away.'

'To your home?' She was at once suspicious.

'Not exactly. But to safety.'

Ellen was not sensitive, or perceptive, or even prudent, but she had a sense of self-preservation of a primitive sort. If she had been an animal, a feral creature (some said she was), she would have known when to run for cover.

'I'd better just tell my friend Maggie where to find me.'

'Later,' said Charley. 'Do it later. Let's bury this meat first.'

They went to the door. Ellen left the door to the garden open to air the house. The refrigerator door likewise.

A cold, damp wind blew out of the trees in the gravel pit, across the garden and through the house.

It blew for two days undisturbed. No one came back to shut the doors, Ellen never thought about them again, no doors opened or closed in her mind.

The wind blew and went on blowing right through the house, bringing in dust, leaves and fallen blossom. Rain made the kitchen floor damp, the refrigerator gave up the struggle to maintain an even low and went into an incessant cycle of freeze and defrost, freeze and defrost.

Maggie tried telephoning Ellen several times. Since Ellen was never a ready or even reliable answerer of telephones it was two days clear before Maggie worried.

'I wonder why she doesn't answer? Or ring me,' she said to Evadne as they piled their cleaning goods into her car. They would be driving off to collect Sophy and Elspeth. John Henry was 'resting' again and so would be joining them, a life-enhancing thought to Maggie. His cheerful good looks were always welcome.

She repeated the question when she met John Henry.

'You can't wonder about Ellen,' he said. He had been in a one-off TV play with her once. 'You just take what comes.' That was the masculine attitude.

Finally Maggie went round to Oakwood herself. The solitary policeman who watched the façade of the house saw her walk up the drive. He took no enjoyment in protecting Ellen; he was one of those who would like to see her hang.

He meditated on hanging. A good quiet way to go for the right sort of person in the hands (joke) of the right sort of executioner, although a messy business in the wrong ones. Of course, *no* death was totally trouble-free either for those going or those staying behind. Things had to be attended to.

He considered this for a moment as he paced up and down. I am a realist, he told himself, there have to be nasty sides. He was not surprised at his obsessive thoughts on hanging which seemed entirely natural and proper to him in the circumstances. He had even discussed the subject with his wife last night, and although a little startled she had talked back. They were expecting their first child in three months' time, and she was having a lot of trouble with her teeth. This happened sometimes, they had been told, due to a calcium loss. She hoped to have a natural childbirth (no wiring up, no induction and no anaesthetics) and she was attending hypnosis classes to help her towards it. He went with her for the fun of it. A kind of pre-couvade.

The child was only a fiction to him at the moment. A faceless disturbance to his life. One he did not, if he was honest, altogether welcome. Images of the child being born suspended like a candle between its mother's legs, together with pictures of a hanging flitted inconsequentially in and out of his mind. He saw no connection between the two, or with his own life. He ought to have been warned.

He was an early stage case of the sickness that was about in Lukesfield at that time. Many people had it without knowing it.

Maggie had it; Joe had it; Sam had had it; Ellen did not have it. Others, unnamed so far, had it. It was spread by direct contact with the carriers. Or perhaps carrier is not the right word, medically speaking. Active infective agent? Not everyone who was approached developed symptoms; some people had a natural resistance. Some others were so strong in themselves that they could meet the symptoms head on and laugh them off. Yet others busily set about infecting their peers.

A few, an unlucky few, took on board everything. These people developed raging symptoms, sometimes intermittent, but always strong. Such a manifestation is, medically, called florid. These unlucky ones had a full, fine, flowered illness. Most recovered naturally as time went on, but one or two were sick for ever.

For such an adoption of an illness there must have been an inbuilt reason. Either there was a congenital weakness, a disposition to such a malady; or else, some event earlier in life had opened up a wound through which infection could pour.

The young police constable, Edward Clark, was sweating into his tunic and under his helmet. This was, in a way, a symptom of what he was suffering from, in as much as it showed that he was no longer comfortable in his skin.

Maggie came out of the house by the kitchen entrance; she was walking slowly.

'Have you seen Mrs Wylie go out?'

'No.'

He stopped thinking his gallows thoughts and snapped to attention: he knew trouble when he saw it, this was trouble.

Ellen Wylie was gone.

Chapter Six

Miss Lavender, the librarian, had created an exhibition of local history in the entrance of Lukesfield's open plan library. She had assembled books written by local authors on the history of Lukesfield, together with drawings and pictures of the town over the years. A pupil of Gainsborough's had painted a passable oil of Lukesfield parish church with a stream and a broken bridge in the foreground, although the stream was now underground and the bridge long since gone. There was a collection of early photographs; starting before the First World War, with a picture of twenty farm labourers gazing in interest over the side of a horse-drawn brake which was ready to take them on an outing to celebrate the Coronation of George V. The photographs were arranged on three walls and starting with the farm labourers went up to pictures of the German bomber that crashed in Lukesfield during the War, leaving a nasty gash in the gravel pits. The series ended with pictures of the Silver Jubilee of Queen Elizabeth II.

Miss Lavender had considered postponing the opening in view of what had happened in Lukesfield, where the disappearance of Ellen, coupled with the finding of the body of Sam, had produced a sourly angry mood. She consulted Ted Toller who was to have opened the exhibition, accompanying this task with a talk on road-safety precautions. She was going to serve coffee and home-made biscuits (made by the Lukesfield WI) with fruit drinks for the children. A local author, a woman who wrote gothic romances, and who had lately arrived in the district, agreed to remain on display all day. The other local author, a cab driver, would come on later as his professional duties permitted.

To Miss Lavender's surprise Ted Toller said go ahead. He would not open it, but would send a deputy, and come in later himself as he wanted to talk to her.

Angel Lavender was surprised at the number of people who arrived, surprised too that a young policeman had turned up to give the talk on road safety, not realising that life itself (or anti-life, some would say) had picked him for the appearance, using the channel of Superintendent Ted Toller. A year ago Eddie Clark had gone on a special course on Road Safety and the Public, so an element of personal pre-selection had obviously taken place.

He was going to call it chance for the rest of his life, but that was in view of what happened later. 'Poor lady,' he said to himself afterwards. 'Why did it have to be her?' A remarkable question seeing that he had been carrying a knife in his pocket for over a week now, apparently uselessly but he had always been attracted by knives since being a Boy Scout. His wife carried the child; he carried the knife.

Ted Toller, having, unconsciously, picked the aptest man for the job, was talking to his wife, she had come to see him in his office after having been to comfort her best friend, long unhappily married to the editor of the local paper, who had just been uncommonly brutal to her. The two friends had not talked about the beating, it happened so often there was nothing more to say on the subject, but after such an episode Ted's wife often made an excuse to seek out her husband for a dose of his gentle, solid good sense.

Her excuse this time was a sandwich lunch to stop him eating canteen food (much preferred but fuller of calories).

'I wanted to ask you something, anyway.' Dutifully, he tucked the cottage cheese sandwich into a drawer to decay damply. 'This tree-house. It's old, but been done up. Looks as though successive generations of children have had goes at it. Did you know about it?'

Mrs Toller had been born in Lukesfield, and had taught in the Infants' School before marriage, a local by birth, she knew the place well.

'No. But I wouldn't. You see, it's a *class* thing.'

'Go on.'

'My father was the milkman, my mother worked in the baker's shop as a girl, I was brought up in another world. Now the sort of children who would build a tree-house as good as that would have been richer. Gentry. So I wouldn't have known. The friends of little Minnie Cooper didn't know that sort of thing. But I expect if you moved in the right circles you would have heard of it. But I'm sure you're right that it was a *secret* that got passed on.'

Perhaps missing a generation or two, and then being rediscovered. That would be most magic of all.

'So – whom should I ask? Come on now, you know them all better than me.'

'Miss Pettit? Yes. Start with her.'

'And about the child being washed after death? Mean anything to you?'

'A simple cleaning-up operation? No? No, I suppose there is something more. I can't say what.'

'If we knew that we'd know a lot more.'

'Consult a psychologist.'

'I think I will.'

'And try Miss Pettit. She knows everything, the old duck.'

Miss Pettit did not know everything that went on in the mind of Lukesfield children but she knew a good deal because she had planted it there. As an educationalist her dictum was: Free the imagination, live out your dreams. Remember Keats, remember Sir James Barrie. Rich meat for most of her junior listeners, but she believed in not talking down. The dangers of talking up had not occurred to her.

As his wife left with a last word about diets, her husband said: 'Mm? I suppose it was Jane and Harry again, really.'

'Yes. Of course.' They both knew why she had come.

'Nothing we can do.'

'Nothing. Terrible things happen everywhere, why not in Lukesfield?' They were both realists, but good people, so that a lot passed them by.

In Lukesfield, Miss Pettit's grandfather had built the first tree-house when his widowed mother brought the whole clan home from India. It had been used and then forgotten. Overlooked when the gravel pits were begun, then dug out, and the workings left. Now it had come into its own again. A house in a tree in a private place.

But as an old man Frank Pettit had told his grandchild and she had played in the house with her brother, rediscovering it as their secret play place. They opened it, rebuilding where necessary, and extending as their imaginations (and that of Sir James Barrie) dictated. *Peter Pan* had greatly influenced them. Three generations back there was a family connection between the Pettits' Scots grannie and Margaret Ogilvy, mother of Sir James. Roland Pettit died on the Somme, his sister hoped to see his spirit. For her he was always 'The Boy'. She hung around the tree-house a lot, waiting, but he never came. She hadn't the gift. The Ogilvy blood had it, but she was all Pettit, yet she never gave up hoping that she might, one day, 'see'.

Minnie Toller kissed her husband goodbye, departing for the library and the exhibition, because she knew he wanted her to go. Nothing had been said, but some message passed between them without words. She continued to think about Miss Pettit, not because she wanted to, but because she had to.

She and Miss Pettit arrived at the library building together and went in side by side, paired, but not admitting it.

They were almost the last to arrive. One more unit of people would soon turn up, but the big entrance hall and exhibition room was already surprisingly crowded.

In the middle stood Miss Lavender, slightly surprised at her success. Everyone here, and so soon. She was gratified.

After Miss Pettit and Minnie Toller came Biddy Powell with her daughter, Tom Wylie and a group of elder pupils, all keen readers. Early addicts, one might say, of the one vice which Miss Pettit encouraged.

It began to get hot in the room. Children always raised the temperature: they breathed faster, their metabolism was more rapid, they produced more heat.

Miss Lavender switched on the wall fan to make the room cooler. It made a lot of noise without helping much.

Maggie had come early. Evadne had said, no, it was not her

sort of thing, never had been. So Maggie came alone and was soon merged in the crowd. She could see Biddy, but could not reach her, and Joe was the other side of the room talking to Arthur Chamberlain. Miss Pettit had her 'readers' hanging around her like bees, and she the queen. Around her neck she wore a very pretty long scarf, spotted and blotched like a leopard. She called it her Maud-Isadora scarf. Maud was her own name, Isadora her preferred one. Wearing the scarf showed her to be happy and her self-image good. This scarf was so well known that it seemed incredible that it never wore out. But, in fact, it renewed itself, or was renewed by her, from a suitable chiffon, so that it was now made of young, strong silk.

It lifted and blew in the breeze from the fan as if alive, a young thing dancing.

A group had come together in the room. Unknowing, unperceptive, they had been singled out for attention. Not all of them knew each other by sight, but underneath it is probable that a kind of recognition stirred, like a wound beneath the skin.

There was a group within the larger group, and they *did* know each other, because they thought they had chosen each other.

This group, although in excellent spirits, had their problems. They had to keep quiet, to behave well, say the right thing, and watch what they were doing. Childhood was their discipline.

Miss Pettit and Biddy Powell stood near each other, Biddy one pace behind. This reflected their relationship. Biddy was acting headmistress, but Miss Pettit was queen.

She smiled cheerfully and happily at all her friends and former pupils. A special wave to Arthur Chamberlain to whom she had taught everything she knew and whose career she regretted. He should have gone to Cambridge to read Literature, but his father, as with *his* father, had pushed him into his own profession. Dentists were valuable, but men of imagination more so. She had a special smile for the young police constable because his mother had worked for her as a cook; she had known him all his life. His father too, a bully if she'd ever seen one. Her hand rested lightly on Tom's head, and she held Mary Powell by the hand. Smiles and nods all round; Maggie and Joe got nothing, she had not taught them.

The two authors stood together for protection, rather awed by the pressures they felt all around them which they were perceptive enough to sense but could not name. Also, by the total lack of interest shown in them by everybody.

'I thought this was our show,' the woman novelist complained. She was plain, not young, but she had presence; anyway, was used to being noticed. 'After all, we were brought here as objects of interest.'

'Doesn't work that way. Might do. Doesn't.' Her friend, the taxi-driver, was detached.

'It's all right for you, darling, but who do I meet, sitting at my word-processor? No one. Eeenie, meenie, mini mo . . . I mustn't go on. But something here smells. One day I shall write it all up.'

'Don't, dear.'

'You may be right. What we have here may be too serious for that.' He saw she was quite in earnest. 'I would not call myself a sensitive woman. By which I mean I have not known telepathy or precognition or anything of that sort. But I have recently had the laying on of hands for a back injury (orthodox medicine never helps backs, have you noticed?) and it has left me with a curious disability.'

'What?'

'It has sensitised me to other people. I *pick* up things. For instance, you might have a pain in your gut.'

She might have picked that up from the smell of peppermint on his breath, he thought.

'Then, when I held the invitation to this party in my hand something very odd happened. I heard a cradle rocking. Or it may have been a bough soughing. A creaking. Certainly it was wood. And with the sound came a smell. I smelt carrion.'

'Oh forget it, dear.'

But she didn't. As she walked about the exhibition she picked up the smell of death again. Once near a pretty woman whom she heard called Biddy, and once near a tall man whom she knew to be Arthur Chamberlain. This both worried and interested her.

She stood near Maggie, introduced herself, and they had a

short conversation. They liked each other, a link had been made.

Miss Pettit took her regal progress around the exhibition, most of which she had seen already because many of the photographs had come from her own family albums. There was a photograph of her brother with a group of his friends, posed with their cricket bats. He had been at Eton; she was proud of that, a King's Scholar, a Prize Fellow of Balliol, but dead too soon.

She leaned forward. 'Is that a spot of blood on my brother's photograph?'

Miss Lavender hurried forward, fussed. 'Oh no, surely not.'

There was a scatter of tiny little brown marks across the face of the photograph, but they disappeared before she could brush them away with her fingers. 'Dust. Silly dust.' Miss Pettit sounded happy. 'A visual illusion.' Blood had fallen on her brother's face, he had died from a sniper's bullet through the throat.

'I didn't see it,' said Miss Lavender, who never had, and never would, see anything.

Miss Pettit moved across the room, her scarf lifting gently in the breeze from the fan. She got too close, the chiffon tails caught in the moving blades of the fan. Her head jerked back sharply, the scarf tightened. Her face went red, her eyes opened wide as if she would not close them. Swaying she dragged at the scarf with her fingers. The fan went round once more, tightening the scarf yet further, before stopping. A burning smell came from the silk. From Miss Pettit's throat issued a noise which no one had ever heard before, a jerky, choking rumble coming from deep inside her.

Then she slid to the ground, pulling the plug of the fan from the wall and dragging it down on top of her.

Miss Lavender had given three piercing screams, as people rushed forward. 'Cut the scarf, cut the scarf.'

The young policeman, Edward Clark, hurried forward, his knife ready in his hand. His hand came out, moving swiftly and neatly, the knife point ready and keen, at some time he must have sharpened the knife like a needle. He ran it round the strangling scarf as if he was trimming a pie, slicing through the chiffon and her throat too. Blood formed as it had around Sam's.

'Cut it down,' screamed Miss Lavender. 'Downwards.'

He looked at his victim, confused. What was he doing?

A babble of people formed around them. Someone fainted, it was Maggie. Joe bent over her, his own face white.

'My hand slipped, my hand slipped,' cried Edward Clark, dropping the knife. He had a dizzy feeling that he had delivered his wife of a child, cut the umbilical cord as if cutting the child from the gallows, giving it life and killing it at the same time.

A woman who worked for the St John's Ambulance Brigade pushed him aside and began to deal competently with poor Miss Pettit.

She was not dead, she did not die, but her vocal cords had been damaged so that she never spoke above a whisper again.

When Miss Catriona Mackenzie, the writer, got home that day she put down her first report of what she had seen. It was to herself, as a kind of aide-mémoire for the book she was to write.

'What happened,' she reported to her notebook, 'was a hysterical phenomenon, I am convinced of it. But what is its nature? Where does it come from?

'If I had not seen for myself I would hardly have believed in it. Not sure I do quite anyway. Something dramatic and "arranged" about it all. The young policeman seemed to *know* what he was doing, and yet, he looked so surprised when he saw the blood.

'I looked round the room and saw that same expression on other faces. Not on *all* in the room, but some. A collection, a group, a coterie, a class.'

She was seeking the right word. She had it, of course, unknowingly. Like so many writers, her unconscious mind was, sometimes, on target, only to be read (as in this case) years later. Talking to herself she often spoke the truth.

Her report went on:

'What makes them a group? Apart from the common look in their eyes, which is only a sign. Or a symptom? Now is that my clue? Are they sick? And if so why? What has infected them?'

This was a fascinating idea, and she played with it for a bit to her own great amusement. Eventually she rejected a mass sickness.

She went over what had happened in Lukesfield. Making a list in her notebook. She loved lists.

Sam, missing, now found bruised and dead, and washed, not exactly from head to toe, but in all crucial areas. The agent: Flight soap powder.

There was the tape, alleged to be with Sam's voice on it, reciting a piece from *Peter Pan* by Sir James Barrie.

Ellen, missing.

Miss Pettit with the ring of blood around her neck, so strangely like the one that Sam have given himself.

A play house in a tree in which generations of children had played.

A whole roomful of people who had looked sorry but not surprised when a young policeman nearly cut Miss Pettit's throat. Not nearly sorry or surprised enough.

These were the facts she set in her report to herself. Too many strange, unpleasant events for one little town like Lukesfield.

Then one word stood on its own in her report:

'Haunted.'

But she crossed this out, being a rational lady, for whom the word haunted did not carry weight.

The next heading was:

What is happening in Lukesfield: fact or fiction?

1. I am imagining it all.
2. I am not imagining it, but the events are not linked.
3. The events are linked and I am not imagining it at all.

Possible reasons for what is happening:

1. A straightforward criminal effort of a group nature. (This I do not believe. No Mafia of Lukesfield for me.)
2. A group murder for reasons of revenge or profit. (I can accept that, but do not find myself much further forward. Who profits from the boy's death?)

3. A murder performed by a group of people but under instruction from another person. (I do not believe this, but it is logically possible.)

In red ink she made a note:

'I hypothesise such a person, but he or she could well exist.'

Then in red ink, again, 'But what is he, she, or it, up to?'

A time gap took place before she made another entry in this report.

'Bad dreams,' she wrote, 'disturbed nights. But at least my dreams, which have been unusual ones, have led me to a thought; namely:'

> Groups may contain smaller groups.
> The smaller group to be the more active.
> Why? Because smaller? Smaller in what way?
> Let me be logical about this:

1. Groups can be smaller numerically.
2. A group may be smaller in height, weight and size. In this case it is not the 'groupness' which is small but the quality of the constituent parts.
3. A secondary group may be both smaller in numbers and smaller in size.

In red ink she added, 'Well, I've bashed that out; I seem to have run through all logical permutations, although I shall never be a logician, but I have covered the ground.'

Chapter Seven

During the next few days, a sense of disaster and fear hung over certain people in Lukesfield. Not everyone experienced it: the postmaster in the village shop felt quite happy. All he knew about what had happened was what people told him. His wife, on the other hand, knew there was worse to come, and went to bed with a mask over her face.

He did not dare ask why: she had cured him of that habit very early in their marriage.

Harry Shaw, angry because his star (only) reporter Joe Archibald had taken the day, the week, off on account of 'sickness', had been savage with his wife, only to find that after the first blow his hand fell back, powerless. A disturbance of the physical laws which had hitherto worked in his favour. It was a kind of miracle. If you could call it a miracle: to him it felt like pain and grief. He thought he had had a stroke. The pain soon faded away, but he never did get back, in his own mind, at least, the full power in his right hand.

Maggie was operating under a dark cloud; she knew now without anyone having to tell her that there was something very wrong: whether it was in the universe, Lukesfield, or in herself, she could not as yet tell.

However, she hid this feeling as well as she could. To David she pretended a physical malaise and put off meeting him, with the result that he decided he had offended her.

Two days after Miss Pettit's throat was cut the police were again in the gravel pits. They were concentrating on the tree in which the tree-house had been found, photographing it, studying it, moving all around.

Understandable enough, Maggie thought as she noticed them on her way to work. She had connected Sam with the tree-house herself. It would need careful police investigation.

It looked to her as though the police team were preparing to dismantle it and lay it piece by piece upon the ground.

A group of children from Pettit's School were standing by watching. Faces were hidden.

'Poor kids,' she thought, 'they probably loved that place. And they've had a rotten time lately.'

One of the children staring at the police hated them for what they were doing. They were at work upon a sacred place.

This child was sophisticated enough to know the word sacred, although not to use it. He was at the front of the little group, he usually got pushed there, as a kind of junior front-man, although he was not a leader. He got the job because he was malleable and gentle with a retentive memory, an amalgam of both his parents. Pretty too, like his mother. Miss Mackenzie had marked him down as a child worth talking to. There never can be a child who looks like that who has not seen more than he should have done, she had thought.

With the child was another, his closest friend and companion, so close were these two that their minds were entwined. Not in any supernormal way, but just that they had read the same books, laughed at the same jokes, played the same games. Together they were like actors who knew the plot and responded to their cues.

But, of course, it meant that what influenced one influenced the other, and upon one child there *had* been outside influence.

'That's our tree,' said the girl.

'Yes.'

'They shouldn't be touching it. Is that what you're thinking?'

'I'm thinking about my mother. I'm always thinking about her.'

'I don't think about mine much.' Reflectively said.

'She knows it.'

They could be tart with each other, these two. He went on: 'You *are* thinking about the tree.'

'Well, they shouldn't be touching it. But it's not *ours*. It could never be that. It's itself. Like an island. Got its own life.' She had well absorbed the spirit of Sir James Barrie as taught by Miss Pettit. 'If it's anyone's now, it's Sam's.'

Then she said, 'Your mother's gone away. I heard your father tell my mother.'

She could follow the conversation he was not having, read the signals beneath the skin.

'She's not dead. I'd know if she was dead.'

Mary put her lips together quietly without answering. She thought she understood a bit more about death and parents than he did: she had cause.

She started to sneeze. Trees had that effect on her.

'I thought you'd been cured of your hay fever.'

'*Pollen* fever. I got over that and started to sleep-walk,' she said proudly. 'But now it's come back.'

'Tree fever.'

'Tree fever,' she agreed. Sometimes he said the right thing unconsciously.

She was cleverer, more perceptive, dominating yet dominated.

'Do you miss Sam?'

'Yes.'

Sam's death had taken them one leap out of childhood. A harsh new world was just visible to them beyond the hole in the curtain. This might be what growing up was.

The conversation beneath the skin began again.

'My mother won't think death's an awfully big adventure. She's not brave. Not brave at all.'

The two policemen in the tree saw the children and wondered if they ought to do anything about it.

'Oughtn't those kids to be at school?'

'On flexitime, I expect,' grunted the other, his feet finding uneasy purchase in the tree trunk which he was investigating. 'It's one of those liberty schools. Do-as-they-like place.'

If Miss Pettit could have heard this and then spoken she would have indignantly refuted it. Dreams are freedom, she would have said, that is all the liberty I give them.

'No kids are that free,' said the elder policeman. So they were out on their own that pair, and could expect punishment when caught. He knew it.

Recognising the woman proceeding forcefully through the trees at that moment, he saw judgement would not be long in coming.

The men were fidgety and uneasy at their task. Kid jobs, as they called them, are never enjoyed. If any murder case ever is – but there is a professionalism always from which pleasure can be extracted, but from which the gloss wears off with children. They sweated a bit, unpleasantly, in their hands and in the armpits, and the back of the neck.

Sergeant Robert Rust, CID felt as though his feet were wet.

'Exterminate them, exterminate them,' he muttered. 'Ever feel that way about kids?' His companion shook his head. 'But then you haven't got any, have you?' And never watched the Daleks either, obviously, judging by the look on your face.

Either his foot slipped or the branch heaved; he thought the branch moved and tipped him off out of malice. It felt like it.

He hit the ground with a thud, one leg pinned beneath him. The pain felt as though someone was taking his leg off from the hip. 'That's me gone,' he thought.

Every sense heightened by pain he could hear the cry of his friend, feel the ground move as feet pounded towards him.

'All right, chum?'

One of his colleagues was kneeling beside him with a concerned face. He tried to say yes, but it came out as a groan. 'No, I'm not,' he managed to say. 'I think I've broken my bloody back.'

'You stay there while I get an ambulance.'

As if he could move. Delicately twitching a toe, agony shot up his back, but there was muscle control. His spine hadn't gone then, it just felt like it. Better not fidget, he told himself.

He opened his eyes. Two children were staring down at him, a boy and a girl. The girl had some matches in her hand, which she was on the point of striking.

My God, he thought, they're going to set fire to me. He wondered what it would be like to have your body broken, then burnt.

'Would you like a cigarette?' said the girl, in a high sweet voice.

He didn't answer, just stared.

'That's what dying soldiers always have. One last cigarette.'

'I'm not going to die.'

She looked at him, her head on one side, her eyes interested. He felt the weight of her interest. Perhaps he was going to die. She looked as though she might know. She was pretty, well behaved, a gentle child, but he had a moment of clairvoyance in which hideously he felt his limbs going up in smoke, smelling like charred tinder.

Then reason told him that it was shock, nothing more. He closed his eyes resolutely against those clear grey eyes, which had him in thrall.

While his eyes were closed Mary extracted a cigarette from his pocket, lit it for him and placed it between his lips. It would have been a moment of high comedy if he had not been terrified. Meanwhile the boy had shinned up the tree and come down again quickly.

'They haven't really touched the tree-house. Just – just checking.'

Tom was a keen watcher of *Starsky and Hutch* when he got the chance, and he knew how the police behaved. Or should behave if TV gave the right clues. 'They can't really do much as the tree grows into the house.'

And the house grew into the tree. What would Sir James Barrie have made of that? Talk about islands that disappear, and woods that appear overnight, here you had a house growing into a tree and a tree becoming a house.

The girl stood looking up at the tree while the cigarette smoked in the policeman's mouth; he didn't seem to be making much effort to puff it. Possibly he was already dead.

She had seen a dead man before; he too had fallen down near this tree, only not quite in the fashion of this man. Her memory of the episode was strange. It came into her mind sometimes as a complete picture, but like a dream. Then little portions took on a complete reality so that she could say, with conviction: I saw that happen. Sometimes she was more sure than at other times.

That is what an act of faith is: she had faith.

She had been pushed to the wood in a chair. Later she had rationalised this by saying: I was in my push-chair. At the time she might not have known the word, but probably that word had been part of her vocabulary. *Now* she understood that there was always a secret pool of knowledge inside one that went unsuspected by adults, but was comprehended by one's peers.

She knew who was pushing her on her walk beneath the trees that afternoon though, that knowledge was clearly fixed. She had known then, she knew now.

Her father had been pushing the chair.

It was a sunny day, he pushed her into the shade, then left her there. She recalled vividly the boredom of being left, the tediousness of looking straight into the same clump of bushes, seeing the same leaves, and the same squirrel running up and down the branches while time was prolonged. The squirrel was free, you were not, being strapped into position in the chair.

Boredom was replaced by fear. You had been left there, and you were going to stay there. For ever. A lost child. Once you have known that particular fear it is always there to be tasted again. Always.

Then from behind came the smell of smoke. A familiar smell, associated with home, and voices talking, and the striking of matches. Not a smell one liked, but homely enough, bringing a moment of comfort.

It was part of the treachery of the hour (felt if not expressed) that this comfort turned to a sharper fear yet. A small, white, smoking object was thrown from behind, to fall on a pile of dried leaves, which almost immediately burst into flame.

You could feel the heat. A little flutter of black ash from the burning leaves spun into your face. You could not move from the chair, but you could twist round in it, shouting for help.

Behind you a figure put something black into its mouth which then flashed with light. After the flash, the mouth was gone, and the face with it. There was no face for you to look at, the body lying on the ground seemed like a doll that had lost its head.

That was your father, that was what you remembered. After that nothing, not going home, not what happened next.

Memory ceased, to come back at odd moments such as now.

During the bustle of getting the injured policeman away and to hospital, the children escaped. They had been noticed, one of the teachers had seen them, a complaint would be made to Biddy, but no one wanted to bother now.

Maggie heard the distant wail of the ambulance as she turned into Pettit's drive. She had not seen the man fall, but she was in time to witness the chastisement of Tom and Mary for running off, when they got back to the school to find Biddy waiting.

'Had to come, can't stop.' Maggie announced, looking sideways at Tom and Mary being led off. 'Had to know, and you can't get a word of truth round here. How is Miss Pettit?'

'Better. Still shocked. She can't talk, of course. But the speech therapist says that there is a very good chance she will do once the stitches are out. Wasn't it terrible? How can things like that happen?'

Maggie did not answer, because there was no real answer. Or not one known to her at that moment. The heavy, dark crown of thorns that seemed to press on her temples lifted a little. It wasn't a precursor to migraine, she knew that quite clearly, just a special kind of misery. If it ever got down to her legs, she would simply cease to walk. Sometimes she thought this would happen. Or the weight would reach her heart, when she would cease to breathe.

But at the moment she was still walking and talking. Inside she knew herself to be immensely tough and strong, so that she might survive whatever doom was overhanging her.

She was an ordinary person to whom extraordinary things happened. Always had been.

'I don't know how things get going,' she said to Biddy, 'but by God, they do.'

'Is there any news of Ellen?'

Maggie shook her head. 'None that I know. What does Nicholas say?'

'Nothing. Says there's nothing to say. He has no idea.'

'I hope she's still alive,' said Maggie sombrely. 'I don't see her as a suicide, though.'

'If I found her I'd kill her myself.'

'No, you wouldn't.'

'No? No, probably not. I expect it's harder to do than one thinks.' Or much much easier, the thought did flash through her mind. 'But she's destroyed Nick. Me too, very nearly.'

'I don't think she killed Sam. Not her own child, she loved him. In her way.' She added, knowing from something David had told her, 'But I think she may have given him marihuana. He may have thought he could fly. It can do that.'

'They all loved *her*.' Biddy spoke with some bitterness. 'Believe it: in spite of everything all three of them, Sam, Tom and Nicky, loved Ellen. I didn't want to believe it. I thought it was a kind of war and I'd win it. But it isn't and I haven't. I've seen Nick's face and I know how he feels. He really loves her, and he'll never get over it.'

Maggie looked at her with sympathy. She knew only too well that love didn't come easily packaged with one's name on the outside and the contents inside neatly labelled for your consumption.

'And that's why I'd like to kill her, because she's so powerful and she's still got everything. Even though she spits all over it. Perhaps because.'

'I don't think she knows,' said Maggie. 'She's quite an innocent really. Not like you and me.'

Biddy did not resent the implication. She understood exactly what Maggie meant, and why Ellen had been wrong for Lukesfield. They understood any prohibition they might be breaking of the society in which they lived. Ellen simply did not notice prohibitions were there.

'Have you had a woman called Miss Mackenzie after you? She talked to me as if I smelt,' said Biddy resentfully. 'And who is she? She seems to be conducting the investigation.' Or writing a book. Or both. 'I wouldn't let her talk to the children.'

She had given Catriona Mackenzie more information than she guessed.

'See you,' said Maggie, swinging off to her work. 'My love to the children.' Some trouble there, she told herself as she drove away, I am sure of it. Like Miss Mackenzie, only in a different way, she was picking up the smell of death about Biddy.

What Maggie did not confide to Biddy was a worry about Joe. He too was not to be seen. Not exactly missing in the way Ellen was, but not around, either. She would talk about it to Evadne, calm, tough-skinned Evadne. Maggie accelerated away to her happier day with Evadne and John Henry. A day not to be touched by anything that was happening in Lukesfield. Life does allow such little respites. Even the tortured drop asleep.

That evening she had a drink with David and they talked about marriage which alarmed and stimulated them both.

In addition he told her that the police believed that Sam had left of his own accord, or at least, freely, and that he had been living in the tree-house for some days. The police had been looking down and not up. Sam's body had probably been bruised as a result of a fall, a series of falls, not a beating. You could draw your own conclusions about how those falls had come about. He had died from suffocation. That was another point to remark. Leaves, clothing too, had been pressed against his nose and face.

Finally they talked about Miss Mackenzie whom they had both met by now and recognised as an influence. But a harmless one, they thought.

And all the time, all around them a terrible feeling was building up in Lukesfield.

Chapter Eight

Arthur Chamberlain, dentist and local historian, did not agree.

His interview had taken place in the office of his surgery, at the end of his day's work. He preferred it so; she would have chosen to see him at his house.

He came home to his tea, took his filled cup from his wife, then sat down heavily in his armchair.

He drank his tea, while his wife waited. She knew to wait.

'She's a very strange lady,' he finally came out with.

'Oh do you think so? I thought she was quite ordinary.'

'Do you believe in witches?'

'No, indeed I do not.' She was firm.

In the pause that followed he held out his cup for more tea and his wife refilled it. He set the cup down on a side table and took up his pipe.

'Neither do I. But she opens one's mind strangely. The direction she pointed me in was one I had not expected.'

'Oh dear. Has she disturbed you?'

'Yes. Horribly.' He put down his pipe, took the cup of tea over to the sideboard where he laced it generously with whisky. 'Some terrible things have been going on in Lukesfield.'

'The whisky will make the tea cold,' said his wife, nervously.

He ignored this suggestion, and drank his mixture.

'You know you hate lukewarm tea.'

'Shut up.'

She blinked. 'I'm sure you have nothing to blame yourself for.'

'Oh, you think that do you?'

'What did this woman say?' She knew it was unwise to push

him, but this question could not hang in the air. 'How did she upset you?'

'She sees through the outer surface of events to what is underneath. Like drilling into a tooth: not painless but necessary. A frightening, all-seeing woman.'

'Oh surely not.'

'She seemed so to me.' He sat with his whisky and tea in his hand. 'Poor Sam Wylie, poor Ellen Wylie, poor Miss Pettit, poor Maggie Chase, poor world.'

He went over to take his bemused wife's hand. 'Poor you, if it comes to that. . . . Sorry, my dear.'

They sat together holding hands.

'I know *exactly* what you feel like,' said his wife. But she did not, had not the least idea, only thought she had from past experience which had been bad enough.

Meanwhile Miss Mackenzie, all unknowing of what she had achieved (for it was an achievement), had succeeded in visiting all of what she called the 'scenes of the crime'. She plodded around the gravel pits, visited Pettit's School, and gained entrance (not legally, but safely) to Oakwood, home of the Wylies, one day to be home of the administrator of the new asylum, soon to be built in Lukesfield.

Since, in spite of what Arthur Chamberlain had said, she had no paranormal powers nor would have believed in them if she had done, and was, in fact, a solid, down-to-earth observer, she picked up no uncanny vibrations. Instead she concentrated on observing what interesting facts she could. These were few. Oakwood she condemned as a dull house, as she flitted through on her unlicensed tour, but rightly concluded that the people who lived inside had not been happy. Too many possessions and not much joy, she decided as she looked at the playroom the two brothers had shared.

She did not admire the Wylies' taste in interior decoration, or respect Nicholas's collection of antique kitchen and gardening equipment. If he had to collect something he would have done better with match-boxes. Cleaner. And as for the furniture: vulgar. Expensive vulgar, which was worst of all.

But she made notes, and photographed wherever possible,

then went home to see what she had got. She took a photograph of the tree and the tree-house, wondering what she would see when it was developed. But it was just a tree, she could see nothing but a tree.

So Miss Mackenzie went about her task, creating waves of alarm wherever she went. Miss Lavender, in particular, began to rue the day she had invented her; she felt she *had* invented Miss Mackenzie. The Local History Group was temporarily suspended; Arthur Chamberlain had announced he was not going to 'do' it.

They were all on holiday, to some people (Miss Lavender was not one) it felt like that. An uneasy holiday, with Sam dead, Ellen Wylie missing, and Miss Mackenzie on the prowl.

But suddenly, there was work for the High-Lo team. The cleansing unit was much in demand. People who would never have thought of using them were suddenly after their services. Not because High-Lo was getting publicity through Maggie finding Sam (although it was), but through a genuine desire to be cleansed.

Mrs Arthur Chamberlain commissioned High-Lo to clean out the house of her husband's last surviving aunt who was moving into a home for the relicts of professional men.

The house was the old family home in which Arthur Chamberlain had spent his childhood. It was an old house, one of the few truly old houses in Lukesfield, whose cellars were medieval. Here his grandfather had written his account of the death of Martha Littlebody, here Arthur had first read it, here had been formed his obsession with local history.

Dolly Chamberlain tried living in the house when they were first married, but she was uncomfortable in it, and forced a move. She said she didn't like the smell of the old place.

It did smell; Maggie and Evadne both noticed.

'Yes, Dolly Chamberlain said we were to clean out the smell. If we can. Doubt it. Smells like an old smell.' Then Maggie added: 'With a new overlay.'

They started work. Sophy and Elspeth together in the kitchen, Maggie and Evadne as a team upstairs. Most of the furniture had already gone, that which remained, heavy and old, was going to be sold. If anyone fancied to buy it; Maggie herself felt that she would not, valuable though it might be.

The two women talked as they worked. They had come closer together over the past few weeks, now they exchanged half confidences, not needing to say everything to tell all. Evadne's life was so simple and open that she had very little to give, but she offered what she had: the hope of another child. It was then that Maggie talked of what she hoped might be her future, admitting to herself afterwards that she had done it in such a confused kind of way that Evadne might not be clear which man she hoped to marry. There was such a strange atmosphere in Lukesfield these days. It was so easy to fall into confusion. There was such a cold, wicked feeling in the air.

But back to work.

'You concentrate on turning out the cupboard while I do the bed and do underneath. . . . My God, there's a chamberpot. Haven't seen one of those in yonks – empty, I'm glad to say.'

Although with Arthur Chamberlain's aged auntie one could not have been sure.

'Wonder what she's got in the cupboard?'

And then Evadne reached into the darkness, feeling, touching, her fingers stretching out.

Fingers touched other fingers, cold and stiff. She had found the hand.

While they waited for the police to come, all four women sat on the step outside; they could not bear to stay inside the house.

Maggie had produced some brandy from the First-Aid box she kept in the car. There was enough for a nip each. Nerves were steadier, but Evadne was still very white. Sophy and Elspeth had been shocked into an unusual silence.

Evadne said, 'It was a biggish hand. Square. Not huge, but not tiny. . . . Ellen had big hands. I noticed.'

'Yes.' Maggie got the word out with difficulty.

'It's Ellen's hand.'

'Yes, I'm afraid so.'

'Her left hand.'

'Yes.' It was more of a gasp than a word.

'Ellen's dead.'

'I think she must be.' Yes, Ellen must be dead.

When the carcass of Martha Littlebody lost its hand no one knew, but there were many stories about what became of it.

Some said it was thrown to the dogs to be eaten. By means of it, said the faithful of the old church, a miracle had been performed in Evesham: a blind girl had been given her sight again. Equally, a decade or so later a witch in the Wirral claimed she had the use of it when the household of her great enemy died one after the other of a strange infection. She rendering herself invisible by means of the hand too, when her enemies came at her, so that she could never be taken. Later still there was a tale that the hand was seen in Lukesfield, all on its own, lying in the churchyard, and then burying itself in the ground. Arthur Chamberlain had this story from his grandfather. There is no churchyard now in Lukesfield, only the vestigial remains forming a kind of garden around the parish church of St Luke, patron saint of madmen.

Maggie and Evadne had both heard of the hand of Martha Littlebody, Sophy and Elspeth had not.

Not one of the women connected the hand in the cupboard with that hand: it was Ellen's hand. Without question it was Ellen's hand.

By the next day more was known about the hand. Many stories were circulating, some better authenticated than others.

Maggie went straight to the heart of the matter by asking David. He told her that the information to be savoured at present was that the hand could be that of a man or a woman, hands once parted from their bodies being harder to identify than you might think. The hand had been amputated from the wrist by someone with a little surgical knowledge. The operation was not, however, a professional job; it had not come from any hospital or medical centre. None had reported a hand missing.

To Maggie's frantic plea to know if it was Ellen's hand, David said, how the hell could he know, and personally, from all he had heard he thought it was a man's hand.

He sounded abrupt, almost unkind, as if he knew something he did not want to tell her. No arrangements to meet were made between them.

What he knew was still secret information. What he knew but could not tell her was that Arthur Chamberlain, dentist and historian, was missing from his home.

His wife Dolly had missed him a whole twenty-four hours before she reported him gone. She had debated anxiously within herself what she should do, as she spent that first sleepless night alone in their big bedroom. What to do? To do the wrong thing was worse than to do nothing.

He had been gone before and come back. He took these fits upon himself, sometimes. She knew from his voice and his face when what she called 'a fit of the miseries' was due to descend. Such moods were not exactly regular, or cyclical, but they happened, usually clearing up spontaneously. Just once the black devil had settled a dangerously long time on his shoulders. That had been a terrible time for them both. She had prayed it would never happen again.

The first episode of prolonged depression had been kept quiet. A few people had known, but not many. But then they had both been young. Now Arthur was such a leader in the community that everyone would know, and he would mind. Only Dolly knew of the pride and the sensitivity inside him. So she had hesitated.

But even Dolly did not know everything. She had not known what Arthur was experimenting with. That he had a plan, and was following it, she could tell, she knew him so well. She knew what the little chuckles, the looks of satisfaction meant when she saw them, but the exact nature of it she did not know. And she knew better than to ask. His pride again. Better not to touch it.

She could believe that what he was feeling so devious about had gone wrong, that now he was feeling wretched and had fled away to hide. Yes, better leave it for the moment.

Being a good, quiet woman, simple in her relationships, she did not connect her husband's absence with what had happened to Sam or to Miss Pettit.

So although she did not sleep that night, she rested more

quietly than she might otherwise have done.

In the morning she remembered that her husband had kept an occasional diary, and started to look for it. She was interrupted by the telephone ringing.

She would not have found the diary, for the diary was gone. It was with Arthur Chamberlain, wherever he was.

When he had pocketed his diary Arthur Chamberlain had begun to realise that he might be a channel through which a strange wind was blowing. He caught a breath of the wind as it went through him, picking up the smell of Martha Littlebody, a whiff of Sir James Barrie, the pungency of acid rain. He did not pick up these things as clear images, rather as sensations of those with which he had once been connected.

Events happen by means of and through people, he told himself, as he collected his diary and wrote a letter, before leaving his house to go to his surgery on the day of his disappearance. I am an agent. A mover.

He did not ask himself what moves the mover made.

He thought *that* part, at least, he knew. Pride going before a fall, he called it, and it was painful.

None of this Dolly Chamberlain had discovered when the telephone rang. She rushed to answer it.

'Mrs Chamberlain? Brian Shee here.' This was her husband's assistant; she had completely forgotten his existence.

'Oh Brian. Good morning.'

'Yes, Mrs Chamberlain, good morning to you. Could I speak to Arthur?' He sounded worried. 'He hasn't been here today.'

She knew. Well, she could guess. He was still talking, but for a while, she was not listening.

When she heard what he was saying, he was talking about blood.

Blood in the surgery. Not what he'd expect at all. Had there been an accident?

Dolly didn't know. She thought *not* an accident, her mind flew to another more alarming likelihood. Last time Arthur had not wounded himself so desperately, much more of a mock slashing, this time he might have done real damage.

Dolly's mind was not big enough to take in all the terrible possibilities that life was offering her at the moment.

Dolly Chamberlain's mind was so full of love for her husband that she could only take in his predicament. She was thinking about the blood; she did not have visions of blood stretching in bands across her eyes, as Maggie Chase had done, or smell it, or feel it bounding inside her head as Joe Archibald had, but she saw it in a severely practical way. She saw blood in the basin at her husband's surgery, washed away, but leaving tiny traces of pinkness where it had once been.

Brian Shee was still talking, now he was going on about drugs. A quantity of local anaesthetics and pain-killing drugs was missing. A careful check was kept on every drug of this nature, so he had known at once how much was gone. This was worrying him.

Did he say something about the police, or was it Dolly's own voice?

'Yes, the police,' she gasped out. 'We must get on to them. You do it, please. Then ask them to call on me. . . . I don't feel very well.'

Brian's voice ceased abruptly, and she heard the young nurse the practice employed speaking to her over the telephone. 'Sit down, Mrs Chamberlain. Put your head between your knees if you feel faint. I'm coming right over.'

The police found Arthur Chamberlain's body leaning against a tree in the gravel pits. The tree was not *the* tree, the old oak of the tree-house where Sam had played, but as near as could be managed. Much nearer would have been to court premature discovery by the police who were still paying a certain attention to that tree. But he got as near as he could.

He had died peacefully from administering to himself an overdose of an anaesthetic drug into a vein. There was a letter, as well as his diary, in his pocket. He had one hand in his lap, and the stump of the other neatly bandaged and tied up in a plastic bag. On both arms were several slash marks as if he had had several abortive attempts at the cut. Before going off to kill himself he had taken his last two hypnotherapy treatments, one with a child, a child from Pettit's School.

After treating the child, he sat down to compose a letter. This took some time and much pain.

Then, having finished his letter, he put a profound dose of local anaesthetic into his left wrist, cut through skin, fat, flesh and bone to amputate it, bound the stump, and went off to deposit the hand in a cupboard so that it should be lost. He was greatly shocked, but mobile.

After this self-conscious parallel with Martha Littlebody, he went to the gravel pits, propped himself up against a tree and took the rest of the drugs he had with him.

So the hand Evadne had found was his, not Ellen's.

Copies of his letter were soon in the hands of selected people. His diary also became known.

Before long a version of it was all over Lukesfield. Reactions varied.

Chapter Nine

Maggie saw a copy of his letter of confession that David smuggled to her. Joe Archibald obtained one in the course of his duties on the newspaper. Miss Mackenzie got a photocopy by judicious use of bribery. Thus all important centres of communication in Lukesfield soon knew what he had said.

I am guilty, Arthur Chamberlain had written in his letter, his apologia for death. And for his life too, for that matter. Clearly he thought his life needed some explanation.

I alone am responsible for the terrible things that have been happening in my beloved Lukesfield. I did not realise at first the harm I was doing. People do not speak of things openly, so much went on in secret before I knew. But when I learnt how the boy Sam had gone, I began to suspect my own guilt. When Miss Pettit's throat was cut, a terrible conviction fell upon me. I could see it all, and see what a terrible thing I had done.

As he had written, hand shaking, he seemed to hear his old teacher, Miss Pettit, speaking over his shoulder: Write clearly and shortly. Get your meaning across without fuss. Be precise.

Stage One: I developed the use of hypnotism as a pain reliever and as a substitute for anaesthesia in my dental practice. I found I have a natural gift for it. Or so I thought. Pride, pride.

Stage Two: I extended my work to relieve the symptoms of migraine, hay fever, blood-pressure. This went so well that one or two doctors sent patients to me for preparation for childbirth. Some great success.

Stage Three: In stage three, he wrote bleakly, *I got ambitious. Too ambitious as I now see. Unwise, with it. Because I was anxious to have a good regular attendance at my Local History sessions I made the suggestion to all those patients who came for hypnosis that they should attend. They must attend.*

Most did so. My command worked. I had a captive audience. I was surprised; I think Dolly guessed, in her way, but she said nothing and I never told her. I loved what was happening. It was like drinking honey. Better than wine.

Arthur Chamberlain had paused here in writing his confession while the spirit of his old schoolmistress prompted over his shoulder: Get on with it, Arthur, get it out, get it over. Because I am part of this, she was saying.

So he wrote:

I began to stir up their minds; I felt I had the power to do it. Miss Pettit said that the great fault of our educational system was that it did not liberate the mind. The imagination must be used, she said. Give it exercise.

So, to the other instructions given under hypnosis, I added a command: Use your imagination, make it work.

I laid down the lines on which it could do so, lines which appealed to me.

To adults, I said: Concentrate on the history of Lukesfield and the story of Martha Littlebody.

Oh my precious man, thought Dolly Chamberlain as she read it, as if that were all. She knew, instinctively, that it was not.

Not enough of an answer there, decided Miss Mackenzie, reading her illegal photocopy.

Joe said to himself: he hasn't asked himself what got into *him*. Why *he* did what he did. Not the right questions at all. Or not enough of them.

Maggie put her finger straight on her own worry: well, it explains some things. A lot. My moods, visions, whatever they were. I'd be glad to blame those on Arthur Chamberlain. I should have stuck to migraine. . . . I was tuned in to Sam. Was he having blood dreams, too? Or was I having them for him? Something went to and fro between us, but who to blame? Just my imagination? I'll accept that. My imagination prodded into life by Arthur Chamberlain. I'd be glad to accept it. But is it all?

A touch of telepathy then? You could believe in telepathy.

It was what she had always said: she was an ordinary person to whom extraordinary things were happening. They were all of them ordinary people to whom extraordinary things were happening.

The police added Arthur Chamberlain's letter and diary to the archive they were building up, made arrangements for an inquest in due course, and continued their investigations. Arthur Chamberlain's diary, the diary of a sick, depressive mind, had added to the details of his letter. His obsession with the past, with the story of Martha Littlebody in particular, was recorded there. As was his excessive esteem for the works of Sir James Barrie, inculcated by Miss Pettit.

Arthur Chamberlain was a suicide, and without doubt had been up to some strange things, but Sam Wylie had not died because he thought he could fly, he had been smothered.

Murdered, and then washed clean. You had to get back to that, Chief Superintendent Ted Toller told David who told Maggie, and reminded her that Ellen Wylie was still missing.

So the burden of informed opinion was that Arthur Chamberlain was not responsible for everything that had happened in Lukesfield.

Chapter Ten

Now that Arthur Chamberlain was dead and the channel of communication which he represented was closed, another channel opened. This joined Catriona Mackenzie and Maggie Chase. It was a conduit, a healing passage through which the sources of order were seeking to re-establish themselves. Goodness was struggling to restore what had been broken.

This was a view Catriona later took herself. Or provisionally, bookwise, as she said cynically, knowing all the time she might, just might, be telling the truth. It was a frightening thought for a lifelong reasonable woman; that she might be directed by a providence.

She continued her study of the case, the police continued theirs. Both had their advantages.

The police had their murder team with its back-up of technicians and scientists; they had their professional expertise; they had manpower. They had also the calm common-sense of Ted Toller, they had the benefit of his essential goodness. Against them they had a deadness of the imagination which allowed them to see only what they wanted to see.

But Miss Mackenzie on her side had plenty of imagination which she encouraged professionally, giving it daily exercise like a dog. Lukesfield brought out in her a kind of mental hyper-activity which she had never known. She was one of the few who actually benefited from the atmosphere in Lukesfield as it then was. What she had on her side was an energy that took her on her investigative course like an armoured column. What she lacked in professional detective skills she made up for with a practical, speculative mind which could create pictures, worlds, universes. She was great on hypotheses. She visited everyone in the case, talked with them.

Miss Mackenzie was pretty well aware that she was looking for different things from the police in her investigation and therefore finding different things.

The police were not aware of her at all.

All those in contact with Catriona Mackenzie began to speak freely to each other about what had gone on in their lives. Maggie told Joe about the bloody visions; Joe responded with the story of his own anger and agony. Mary Powell told her mother that she remembered seeing her father shoot himself. Biddy could hardly believe it.

'You were not two years old.' She repeated, 'not yet two.'

Miss Pettit alone said very little, but she wrote an account to her oldest friend of how she had brooded over her brother's death in war, always seeing his face in the strangest places.

The police knew nothing of all this, and no one told them. David could have told Ted Toller but the relationship between him and Maggie was still very close and private to him. In any case, it was not the sort of information a man like Ted could use, his mind could not chew on it. He had enough difficulty digesting the Chamberlain letter.

Thus it was obvious that the police investigation and Miss Mackenzie's were working on two different planes. The police were investigating the death of an autistic boy under mysterious circumstances, discovering practical clues (such as the washing, the way he was smothered) which were leading them to suspect a certain person. Miss Catriona Mackenzie was heading for other worlds.

But there was one point where the two investigations met: on the subject of hypnosis. Both sets of investigations wanted to know if hypnosis *could* do what Arthur Chamberlain claimed he had done.

(For that matter, the argument raged in Lukesfield between those who thought Arthur Chamberlain should have been hung, drawn and quartered, and those others, the healthy and the uninfected with good teeth, who thought it was a shame he had killed himself for what could not possibly have happened. Not the way he said.)

The most famous expert on hypnosis in southern England happened to be attached to the mental hospital whose arrival in Lukesfield was planned. He was a member of the British Society of Medical Hypnotists, a Fellow of the American Society for Clinical and Experimental Hypnosis, and a Professor in the University of Birkhill. He was also a consultant psychologist to several police forces, including the one which staffed Lukesfield.

In addition Dr Sage and Miss Mackenzie had once corresponded on the subject of extra-sensory perceptions, both in a spirit of cordial open-mindedness, willing to believe, but not ready to be credulous. A relationship between them, not at all extra-sensory, had briefly bloomed, then ended naturally.

When he was contacted by both the police and his old lover, he sent out the same photocopied reply to their questions. He always had a pile of such documents to hand because he got such a questionnaire at least once a week. The questions they asked were the questions the lay mind *always* asked.

He began:

Aesculapius in the fourth century BC probably used hypnotism. There is a long history of using suggestion as a curative technique. So yes, it is respectable. Today it is widely used in dentistry, obstetrics, alcoholism and dermatology. In obstetrical hypnosis the husband is often trained with the wife. Sometimes these hypnotic sessions can be combined with visits to a dentist who uses the technique.

It is a fallacy that no person under hypnosis can be induced to do something that they would not do when awake. It is simply a question of adjusting the technique. Thus, a girl instructed to remove all her garments would probably snap awake. But if told she was undressing to step into a warm bath prepared by her mother she would certainly strip.

So instructions can be conveyed to a subject without the specific will of the patient.

Mood can be changed. Depression may be alleviated; aggressive impulses reduced; phobias helped away. Yes, mood can be altered in the majority of people, what follows will be up to them. But remember, with hypnosis it is not an all or nothing situation.

He added:

It has been put forward that all hypnotism is really self-hypnotism; that what takes place is channelled by the subject, and that the hypnotised person's expectations are important in what is achieved.

He had a few more points to make, such as the fact that although the subject could usually be instructed to forget what had happened while under hypnotism, this could not be guaranteed. Subjects sometimes remembered every detail.

Further, that there is no evidence that hypnotism promotes mind-reading or telepathy, even if there is such a thing.

Finally, he added a note to the effect that hypnotism was a technique, and an art, and nothing about it could be taken for granted.

He instructed his secretary to send out two copies, first class post. On the copy for Miss Mackenzie he scribbled a note:

Oh Katie, Katie, what are you up to in Lukesfield? Stirring the soup as usual?

The soup at Lukesfield was very thick indeed, thicker than was thought, in that short period after the discovery of Arthur Chamberlain's body and before the final outburst. The suicide and confession of Arthur Chamberlain had not lifted the mood at all. Hatred and rancour grew like rank weeds. Anger focussed on one name, then another. Dolly Chamberlain came in for her share till she went to stay with her son. Somehow that protected her. Then it was Nicholas's turn. He walked around with his head down, not looking at people. If Ellen had been there she might have been lynched, that was how it felt. 'For Sale' signs were appearing everywhere. Better to get out, was the implied statement, before something worse happens.

Nicholas asked Maggie to help him sort things out at Oakwood now the house was sold and before the furniture was put in store. He was going to go on living with his mother. They were looking for a place in London.

She was reluctant. 'Can't you ask Biddy?'

'The short answer is No.' He looked at Maggie, who wanted more: Ellen and Biddy were both her friends, she needed to know. 'The funny thing is I'm missing Ellen; I can't stop thinking about her. She's in my mind all the time. I suppose I'm still in love with her. Always was.'

Yes, Ellen, so overlooked when there, had never been more

powerful than when off-stage.

'And Biddy can tell.'

'Of course she can.' Maggie looked at him with scorn. 'And anyway, I expect you've told her.'

'It seemed only fair.'

'Oh you're lovely, absolutely lovely.' Maggie turned away, her face angry.

Nicholas flushed. 'Please.'

'All right, I'll think about it. But it will be a business arrangement. Is that understood? . . . Do you know any more about what's become of Ellen?'

'The police say she went off of her own accord. They've traced a taxi-driver who took her to a station. She had a case.'

'I expect she was running away from you and your accusations that she'd killed her own son.' Maggie was not surprised, David had sketched the same story for her. But who knew what had happened to Ellen after this?

'We still don't know exactly what happened to Sam,' Nicholas reminded her.

Sam had gone away freely; he was dead. Ellen could be dead, too.

'Biddy thinks she might be able to get more out of the children if we give her time,' he went on.

Maggie said, 'Poor old Arthur Chamberlain. We ought to hate him. I think I do.'

'I can tell you one thing,' Nicholas added savagely. 'All copies of *Peter Pan* have been removed from the school library.'

'And poor old Sir James.'

'I personally think Arthur Chamberlain was round the twist and not responsible for anything he did.'

'He meddled,' said Maggie vindictively; there was a cloud over *her* mind. Who knew what other damage the man had done? 'I think Biddy's quite right to listen to the children.'

Nicholas said, answering her tone rather than her words, 'You'll help me with the house then?'

'The removal firm will do it all for you. You don't need me.'

'Personal things, Maggie,' he pleaded. 'Clothes, you know.' Then he said, 'She had a lover; there might be some traces –

signs. I don't want anyone but you to know.'

'What about the police?'

'They know. I said.'

'All right. I'll come.'

Next day by arrangement they met at Oakwood. There was the usual Ellen-made confusion, compounded by a thorough turnover from the police.

'I'll do the toys, you do the clothes.' Nicholas had brought with him two large trunks together with a selection of boxes.

The house smelt clean now. Someone, not Maggie's outfit, had cleared away all dead food and scrubbed around with heavy disinfectant. It didn't smell like Nick and Ellen's house any longer, more like an institution. Gone was the smell of cigarette smoke, drink, Ellen's scent and the occasional stink of blood.

Maggie felt lonely. 'I miss Ellen too, I know she could be a pain, but she was here, real and loving. I didn't realise how she counted. I thought I was helping her, but she was the strong one.'

Nicholas nodded.

'I know that now. I keep sending silent messages: Come back, Ellen. But she doesn't seem to hear. I thought of putting an advertisement in the papers: Come Back, Ellen. But she never reads them.'

If she's where she can read them, thought Maggie as she silently got to work. They separated to go about their tasks. meeting at intervals, usually by the back door where a great pile of rubbish was accumulating.

At one of these meetings, Nick said, 'I found this.' From his pocket he drew a sheet of writing paper covered with Ellen's large, curving handwriting which got in about six words to the page. 'She seems to have been writing a love letter. I knew she'd leave something around. This isn't the only sheet. She had several boss shots. Perhaps she just liked writing his name.' He pushed the paper towards Maggie. 'Charley. Well, now I know his name. Charley or dear Soul.'

Short-sighted Maggie was peering at the writing. 'No . . . I think it's Charley Soul. I've seen the name somewhere.' She pushed the sheet back. 'She may just have beem writing-in a new pen. I've done that.'

Nicholas laughed. 'Oh screw it.'

'Will you show the police?'

'I'm a lawyer, but I will not.' He tore up the paper and threw it into the rubbish. 'Let it join the rest. How are you getting on?'

'Nearly done.'

There was a great sack of rubbish which they carried together to the bins outside. Maggie was pleased to see that Nick had donated his collection of kitchen and garden antiques to the town tip.

She heard Nick swear as he opened the bin.

'Look here.'

He was holding out a green plastic bag with white handles, emblazoned Friends of the Green Earth. The bag was stained and greasy with muck from the bin. Before Maggie's eyes he tipped it up, to pour out on the floor before her a mink stole, a white fox jacket and a scatter of jewellery, pearls, diamond earrings, a bracelet of pale stones, and a couple of rings. Everything was stained and greasy, too.

'Ellen's,' he said. 'Everything valuable I ever gave her. Just dumped.' He was almost in tears. He held up the white fox: 'Look, she's even tried to cut this up. See what she thinks of me – just hates me.' He threw the fur from him in disgust. 'They'll all have to be cleaned.'

Maggie picked the furs up, thrusting them back into the bosom of the Friends of the Green Earth. 'I'll drop these at the cleaners. The jewellery is up to you.'

Maggie took the furs home with her, wondering if she had seen something in the episode that Nick had not. He had seemed oddly blinded to the implication.

That night Maggie had a vivid nightmare. She dreamt she was in a room with Sam's killer. She was stretching out her hand to push him away, but his face came closer and closer. As she touched it she felt it was made of cardboard, the whole face was painted paper. It was a mask, but even the eyes behind that seemed to stare at her were not real. She rapped one with a fingernail: it was hard and dead. Nevertheless the cardboard figure bore down upon her, seeing her through eyes that were not there.

She woke up sweating and pounding on the bed-head, glad to be awake, out of the nightmare, back in the world. All the same, it was a relief that it was an ordinary, commonplace nightmare, the sort of dream normal people had, and not one of those daytime horrors that had hung about her. True, the migraines had returned with renewed force, but she regarded the headaches now as the lesser enemy.

Maggie switched on the light, and considered her dream. Yes, nasty, and it wasn't true you could not dream in colour: she just had. Her mind had been trying to say something to her through the dream.

The murderer was cardboard? So what did that mean?

You think you know the murderer of Sam, don't you? she reminded herself. Your mind is telling you that he is a cardboard figure.

Right, she wasn't disputing it, the murderer *she* had in view was, in a way, a cardboard cut-out. Conscious and unconscious mind seemed agreed.

She settled down again, enjoying the softness of her bed, the quiet of the room. Sleep was hard to come by, though. The murderer would not go away.

Most dreams fade fast, this one did not. The memory of it still hung over her the next day. The dream was prodding her into action, but as so often with dreams was delivering an ambiguous message.

In the morning she left a telephone message for Joe to get in touch with her: it was the best she could do. After that it was up to him.

Then she telephoned David; she told him about the furs in the bag, in the dustbin. To her it seemed important information, she waited to see how he reacted. What she got from him might well be, as it were, the official police line.

He said at once, 'The furs must have been put there *after* Ellen went, and *after* the police searched the house consequent upon her being missing. Otherwise they would have taken them out.'

'I thought that, too.'

'So either Ellen came back, or someone else went into the house with a key.'

'I thought that too.'

He hadn't seen as much in the episode as she had, then. That interested her.

'My advice to you is to ring up Ted Toller and tell him.'

'Will you do it for me?'

'No.'

'Then I'll get Nick to do it.'

'He's probably done it already.'

'Might have done.' But she doubted it.

She began to put the receiver down. If she read David's mind right then the police line was going to be blinkered and unimaginative, and she was away ahead.

Across the telephone line she heard David's voice: 'Don't play detective, Maggie.'

Maggie laughed. He just heard her reply. 'Never.'

That day Charley Soul went to church, not in Lukesfield but in a town not far away. He had always been one of those who thought you were nearer to God in a garden, and so on. Churches, as such, had not figured in his life. He was the preacher not the listener, his gospel was his own.

But now he was troubled. He had acted for the best but in haste.

Since he thought of himself as a wandering preacher spreading his message as he travelled, perhaps he should go on his travels again.

But he knew that he had moved out of a world where his private standards ruled, to a public world in which law existed. It was a shock.

In the end, it seemed you could not escape. He would have to come out and face it.

He went around the church like someone savouring the taste of a new food. He liked the faint smell of incense, the musty smell of the pews; he liked the light through the coloured windows. There were religions other than his own private one. Life might be changing for him.

Without knowing it he was saying to himself what Maggie had felt: that in the events at Lukesfield a moral law had been broken, and that punishment was not only inevitable but had been happening for some time.

Maggie took the furs with her, tossing them into the boot. 'Those will have to go to London, preferably to the furrier who supplied them,' she thought. 'No good trying locally. I've never owned a fur, can't fancy wearing the skin of dead little animals, but these are good pelts. You can't toss them into the local launderette.'

Joe was waiting for her at the step of his mobile home, which was backed by an open field grazed by ponies and fronted by an ancient church.

'I got your messsge. Here I am. I've been waiting. What is all this about? I really ought to be working.'

For an answer Maggie opened the car boot and showed the furs. 'Look.'

He recoiled.

'What a terrible smell.' His face had gone white.

'Is the owner still alive?'

'How should I know? Shut them up. They smell dead. I hate dead animals.' He was shaking.

'I know you do, Joe. We all do. It would be better to talk inside.'

'What have we got to talk about?' Joe asked. 'I thought things were subsiding. Settling down now Arthur Chamberlain has gone. You have your migraine and I have my allergies but the moods have gone. Our minds have cleared. I had terrible angers. All right now. I hope the same for you too. That man put a hook in us but it's gone. We're all much more normal.'

'In one of those black moods did you kill Sam?' demanded Maggie. 'You see, what the furs in the bin spelt out to me was your presence. They spoke out loud and clear. I knew Ellen had a lover. She called him Charley. I didn't know who he was. But I guessed that Ellen and Charley had been together when Sam went missing. I thought the two of them together might have killed Sam. A lot of people thought as much. But in the end I couldn't believe it of Ellen. . . . But that still left Charley. Only I didn't know who Charley was. He could be a joke, or an invention. A kind of preacher man, Ellen called him. A visiting evangelist? But you could never tell with Ellen.' She said, 'And then I remembered you and your crusade, what you thought about the world and the way we treat it.'

'The furs in the bin was a stupid thing to do,' said Joe. 'But I've always hated dead things.'

Maggie said; 'The stupid thing to do was to make me your friend yet not be honest. How could you, Joe?' Angrily she added, 'Or whatever your real name is.'

Joe looked away. 'It's a shame about Charley Soul. He was an awfully good little beast while I had him going. The right name for the right man.'

'When we went looking for Sam, you knew we were looking for a dead boy, didn't you?'

Finally, Joe said: 'Yes.' It took him a long time.

'Did you kill him?'

'No, no, I didn't.'

'Nor did Ellen?'

'As far as I know. I don't know who killed Sam. You know as much as I do.'

Maggie pressed on. 'And Ellen? What have you done with her?'

Joe took a deep breath. 'I thought she'd be attacked in Lukesfield. Everyone was out for her blood here. You know they were. I took her away. She's with my stepmother. I do have one. She can come back any day she likes.' He gave a brief smile. 'Between you and me, I hope she will. She has been no easy guest.'

Part of the healing process initiated by Catriona, carried on by Maggie, was under way. For some like Joe it would be complete, for others there would be, at best, a time of remission.

Maggie started to talk first. 'We don't know who killed Sam yet, do we? It has been a horrible time in Lukesfield. I'm not imagining all this, am I? Others have felt it too?'

'Is it all Arthur Chamberlains's fault? Did he bring it all about by what he did? Is it possible that hypnotism could do so much?'

'It was bloody dangerous,' said Joe. 'I had a bad time whether it was his fault or not.'

'Perhaps it was not his fault entirely. Perhaps he could not help himself' said Maggie, speaking quietly, almost to herself. 'I have felt things beyond us reaching out to touch us, to make us act. Things from the past, perhaps. . . . He was so obsessed by Martha Littlebody, as was his grandfather. Supposing she was buried here, can the dead touch the past?'

'They do it all the time?'

'Yes, through what we know of history and so on. But directly, malevolently, personally, as an act of vengeance?'

'How can that be?' said Joe. 'I accept hypnotism, even telepathy, but I don't go beyond it. I respect and believe in the living world with its rules and that's it.'

'I'm not saying I believe in more,' said Maggie. 'I am open-minded.'

'So?'

'It means we are dealing with different realities. My reality, Arthur Chamberlain's reality, your reality, Sam's. All a bit different, all co-existing.'

'Is there no absolute reality then?'

'Now you are winding me up in a ball,' said Maggie good-humouredly.

Meanwhile, the police investigation, which was operating on a different plane from that of Maggie and Catriona, and with a firm grasp of its own reality, had made progress.

In their world horror had its proper place, they knew all about it, and had no need to invoke supernatural intervention. In their world a mother had burnt her child on its arm with a cigarette because it cried, while a husband had crippled his wife by breaking her pelvis. Three people had become cinders because a neighbour had thrust burning petrol through their letter-box. This treatment had been handed out because the husband had run over the neighbour's cat and left it to die. His wife and son had nothing to do with this, did not even know, they were just unlucky.

In such a world where this, and worse, could happen, they thought they had enough trouble without looking around for any more. Using their own techniques they were approaching a solution. Not to the horrors of Lukesfield, which for them did not exist, but to the murder of Sam Wylie. So using what came naturally to them they identified the murderer.

Even the motive they had little trouble about. In fact they could suggest more than one. Their expert psychologist's advice informed them that the motive would be mixed.

This was indicated by the washing of the body, which he said would be in expiation. In part. Possibly, also, as a ritual to confirm the association of the group.

Group?

Yes, group, but it need not be a group murder. It would only have needed one small pair of hands to finish the boy off.

The police knew who this killer was, but they were nervous about their legal position. They must not only act well, but be seen to act well.

So they moved slowly.

Many people had a guess about the direction in which the police were moving, but got it wrong. They guessed the way they wanted to guess.

The first action of the police before beginning to wind the case up was to collect Ellen from where they had traced her, and then pull in Joe. They had not found it beyond their power to trace her, but had kept their enquiries secret. Both of them were at the Lukesfield police station in that state known as 'helping with enquiries'. Most of Lukesfield assumed a charge would soon follow. It was what they expected of Ellen, although Joe was a surprise.

Maggie hurried at once to the police station to try to see Ellen and Joe: she was refused. She thought that, distantly, she could hear Ellen screaming, but she might have been wrong. Perhaps it was Joe. Or just a voice in her head.

Visions of blood had certainly left her but she did not feel cheerful. Too much seemed about to happen. She telephoned David to ask for help in seeing her friends, but bluntly he told her to keep out.

Maggie guessed that both she herself and Miss Mackenzie would shortly be interviewed by the police to see what they knew: the two women agreed not to meet for the time being.

There was no point, they felt, in inflaming the bad feeling now shown on every side in Lukesfield. Joe's mobile home had been vandalised in the night; an attempt was made to burn down Oakwood by throwing a milk bottle full of petrol at it, but it was thwarted by Nick who had gone back to living there to protect his property. The house was sold, but contracts had not yet been exchanged. Pettit's School was given a police guard. Biddy Powell had been questioned once again by the police, but she had expected this as soon as she heard that Ellen and Joe had been taken and was prepared. She wondered how long Pettit's could remain open as a school; this was a deep worry, she had a lot of money and hopes invested in the school. Perhaps Miss Pettit, who had always been such a rock, would know the answer. She was due to visit the old headmistress in the nursing home where she now lived, that evening. Since she could neither leave Mary alone nor take her with her, she asked Maggie to come over.

On the telephone, she said frankly, 'There are other people I could ask, but you are the only one I can trust, you're one of us, one of the group.'

Groups form and take shape all the time; this group was made up of those who had suffered through the troubles of Lukesfield.

'Practically a founder member,' groaned Maggie. 'Right, I'll be over.'

She was glad enough to leave her own house, empty and neglected as usual, to drive to Pettit's. For a moment she felt a gust of nostalgia for the days when she had run the best lingerie shop south of the Thames and her only worry had been what red meat to cook for her husband's dinner. No, that was not being honest: there had always been worries, and this was what had come of them, an empty house and an anxious woman.

As she drove she passed the gravel pits, lit by an evening sun. She turned her head away so as not to see it, as she always did now. There were some things she did not wish to remember, although remember she must.

She was still in a state of confusion about Arthur Chamberlain. Thoughts floated in and out of her mind. Thus:

I forgive him as a person. But what he did was unforgivable.

It upset a balance. Broke a moral law. Why did he do it really? The influence of Martha Littlebody, that's one answer. There must have been many such deaths as the Littlebody one, and they do not set up a haunting, a horror. Why that one?

The intense anger of the woman, perhaps? Striking through the soil.

But she guessed that the nature of the universe was not such. And, in any case, no one knew where unlucky Martha and her child had been buried. It was reasonable.

Beneath the oak tree on which so much violence had centred, a selection of bones lay deep in the soil. The roots of the tree grew in and around them. When the area was eventually cleared and the remains of the tree felled, these bones were discovered, then to be judged human and some three hundred years old.

Maggie, as she drove on, carefully not looking, could hear another dead voice in her memory. She had no idea what Martha Littlebody's voice would have been like; she supposed an untutored countrywoman's voice suited to her position, but not the voice of the court, rustic but polite. When she shouted her anger it would have been in a voice that most of her auditors would have felt at home with. A voice Shakespeare might have used for one of his tragedies.

The voice that Maggie heard was a soft voice with a lowland Scottish accent. 'When I was little I ettled to go ben,' it said. 'Events in the next room have always been to me a mystery and a romance.'

She did not know what the words meant, or where she had come across them, but they were real. A real voice had spoken them.

Then the same voice spoke the words that Sam had used: 'To die will be an awfully big adventure.'

Only a romantic who had a gothic view of death could use such words. It was an adult voice, and a monstrous lesson to teach to a child. Had Sir James known that in the end?

Maggie knew something was wrong as soon as she drove up to Pettit's.

To begin the door was wide open. These days no one in Lukesfield left their door open.

Once inside, standing in the spacious entrance hall facing the main staircase, she knew that what was wrong was very wrong.

Maggie called out: 'Biddy, I'm here. It's Maggie. Where are you?'

No answer. No echo even for her voice in a house that usually sang with echoes. Her words seemed to sink into dead sound.

At least the house was full of light. It was still daytime but the central light was on in the hall, while from a side room more light shone.

She went towards that room. She knew it was the main school dining-room; she'd cleaned it, polished it and eaten in it in her time. A room she knew well, a happy, lived-in room.

Biddy was sitting slumped at a table near to the door with her head in her arms. She looked up as Maggie came in, but for a moment did not seem to see her.

Her face had no colour, nor much expression. She acts like a woman who had been hit on the head, thought Maggie. 'Are you all right? You look terrible.'

'Can you see? Is it very dark in here? I turned on all the lights.'

'No, it's full of light.' But there was a positive darkness outside the light, waiting to get in, she could sense it. 'What is wrong, Biddy?'

'*Feels* dark,' Biddy whispered. 'Cold, too.'

'It is cold.' Maggie sat down beside her friend, and put her arm around her. 'What's up?'

'I won't be going to see Miss Pettit.'

'No, Biddy. I understand that. . . . But why not? What's gone wrong? I can see you've had a shock.'

There was silence.

Biddy took a deep breath, and then let it out with a shuddering gush of breath. 'It's my child.'

Maggie gripped her friend harder. 'Tell me – is she ill? . . . She's not *dead*.'

Biddy seemed to have difficulty in taking in what was said to her. After a pause she said, 'No, not dead, not ill. It's what she's done.'

There was something that had to be said, and Maggie said it, with some force. 'Where is she *now*? Where is she?'

Biddy said vaguely, as if this bit was not important, 'Oh here, in the school. Don't worry. She's safe.'

This from Biddy who had treasured her child, and in a house where all the signals were so baleful, chilled Maggie more than anything so far.

'So – what is it?'

Biddy said, 'I don't know how much you know about hypnotism?'

'I know what we all know now.' Maggie spoke with some bitterness.

'Oh yes, I forgot, for the moment, that you were one of those.'

Maggie nodded: one of *those*. Was it going to be a brand for ever?

'Apparently it's always different. Sam could not really *be* hypnotised, not by Arthur Chamberlain. But Mary took it beautifully. Really helped her. Afterwards the hypnotist instructs you to forget the whole session.'

'I *know*.'

'Just sometimes this does not work: you have total recall. That happened to Mary. The last time she had a session she remembered everything. Afterwards she told Arthur Chamberlain. At once. It was after that he killed himself.'

Maggie waited; Biddy sat silent. 'Well, go on.'

'Mary told him, and has now told me that she knew all the time that Sam was hidden in the tree-house. She and some other children, Tom was one of them, helped him. She told Arthur Chamberlain that, influenced by him, they were acting out *Peter Pan*. Sam thought he could fly.'

The drugs his mother may have given him could have helped this idea. Did Sam know what he had taken, and perhaps liked it?

'But–' Maggie started to say. But Biddy read her thoughts.

'Although Arthur Chamerlain could not hypnotise Sam, Mary *could*. He loved her. Do anything she wanted. Be anything. He believed in her. He was happy being a bird or whatever he thought he was. He tried to fly, fell.' A fall from grace? 'Mary and Tom dragged him to where you found him. It was an accident, Sam died by accident.' She looked at Maggie fot assurance. None came.

Maggie said: 'Where is the child now?'

'In my sitting room. I didn't want to alarm her too much. The police have telephoned me to say they are coming here to question me and Mary. So they know. That's why I started asking her questions. I should have done it before.'

The police were also on their way to question Tom and his father Nicholas, also a couple of other young children from Pettit's together with their parents. They saw things differently from Biddy Powell.

'I should have questioned Mary before,' repeated Biddy.

Years and years before.

Biddy had not seen it coming. Did not see now what was going to hit her.

She whispered, 'They washed Sam's body, and laid him out. Wanted to make him clean and tidy. I think that's terrible.'

What had really happened was even more terrible.

Maggie said, 'I don't think you ought to have left her alone.' She got up; she knew there was darkness waiting for them outside. 'Let's go and find her.' She led the way to Biddy's private sitting room. Usually this room was a pleasant one full of sunlight and warmth with bowls of flowers everywhere. There were still plenty of flowers, but they were all dead. The room smelt of stale water. Biddy seemed oblivious. It was doubtful if she had looked at her sitting room for days.

The room was empty. A cat slept in one corner of an easy chair, enjoying a last patch of sunlight. A small canary swung on its perch in the window, looking at them with bright, shallow eyes. But of Mary there was no sign.

'She might be in her bedroom.' Biddy hurried off, followed by Maggie.

Mary's bedroom was as bare of Mary as the sitting room had been.

'She hasn't been here at all,' said her mother decisively. 'The room's too tidy. Mary is not tidy.' She caught Maggie's alarm and she was anxious. 'I don't understand. I left her reading. She seemed quiet. She knew I was upset but she was calm.'

The apartment set aside for Biddy's private use was not large, four rooms in all, with a bathroom. The two women went through them quickly, then came back to the sitting room.

'Where else?' Maggie spoke. 'What about the school itself?'

'Locked. The communicating door is locked at night.'

'Where's the key?'

Biddy rushed across to her desk, where she pulled open a drawer. She started opening other drawers, turning over papers. 'Perhaps I put it somewhere else. No, I *always* put it there in the drawer.'

Maggie left her behind to run towards the door to the school. The door was closed, did not yield to her, looked as solid as oak.

Biddy arrived to push at the door too.

'It's locked the other side.' Maggie was peering through the keyhole. So Mary had taken the key, and must be inside. 'How can we get in? What window?'

She had washed them often enough to know that the easiest window would be in the Junior room. To get there you had to pass the barred windows of the small gymnasium. No use trying those.

Maggie ran past, not looking, with Biddy catching her up fast.

Then she heard Biddy scream. Biddy was staring through the gymnasium windows. Maggie went running back to her.

Through the barred windows she could see into the room to the further wall which was lined with horizontal bars.

A small figure was suspended by the neck from the top; she could see it hanging there, twisting very slowly round and round.

As she looked Maggie knew she was looking at the final horror of Lukesfield. She never remembered breaking open the Junior-room window, but she must have done so because later there was blood on her hand and arm and she had stitches put in at the hospital.

She did remember Biddy frantically clawing at the skipping-rope round her daughter's neck. She remembered having grabbed a great kitchen knife to cut Mary down. Biddy was screaming at her not to cut the Mary's throat. They were quarrelling, almost fighting over the child's body. It was ludicrous and terrible at the same time.

'She's alive,' Maggie said. 'I can feel her pulse.' It was thready and bumpy, but distinctly there.

But looking at the child, eyes closed, face bruised and bright with blood under the skin, she wondered how long the brain could manage on diminished oxygen and if there would be brain damage.

Biddy pulled herself together to summon an ambulance and then sat there nursing her child. 'My darling, my darling,' she was saying, 'nothing is your fault. Forgive me, my dearest, my darling, my child. It was all that terrible man, and I took you to him. Mummy's to blame, my darling, I'll look after you. Nothing is your fault – an accident.'

The police had come to another conclusion, they saw things differently. In their hands the forensic evidence told another story. They had their voices, too, speaking to them saying hard practical things, This is what their voices said:

Sam's death was not an accident; he had not died as a result of his fall, he'd been smothered by small, eager hands. One pair of hands had held a brightly coloured pad over his mouth till he stopped breathing. The fibres matched those of the overalls worn by the children of Pettit's School. Then these hands, with other hands, had washed him. Four children were involved; Tom, Mary and a younger pair of twins. These last were too young to be held responsible.

Murder by his peers was their verdict.

Maggie sensed a change in Lukesfield as soon as the news was out. Relief of a kind, but not a happy relief, one could not call it that, more like the feeling when the symptoms of a dread disease are confirmed and the suspense is over but the pain is about to begin. The affair was kept as discreet as possible, so not everyone knew the details, but amongst those who did a sick quietness was the reaction. Children. Children in Lukesfield being like that: it was hard to take. Naturally, rumours spread.

Among the group that had formed, willy-nilly, around Arthur Chamberlain the relief was greatest. Some few of them suspected that it would never be over, and that their minds would carry it within them for ever, like an extinct volcano waiting for new life to erupt.

The other, smaller, inner group of the children could not communicate since they were being kept strictly apart. Tom was living with Nicholas in a furnished flat on the edge of London. His grandmother had refused to keep him any longer, she said she couldn't bear to keep looking at him. Ellen had joined her husband and remaining son. Somehow they felt happier together.

The twins had been sent off to different relatives and were not allowed to correspond or telephone. But they showed no signs of wanting to do so, perhaps it was a relief not to be together.

Mary Powell was in hospital. She had been resuscitated successfully, brought round from her suicide attempt to face life. But she had a high temperature which defied the doctors attempting to bring it down. Unable to make a diagnosis they called it shock. Maggie wondered about the child's mind.

Maggie too was in shock, her symptoms were nightmares in which she saw Mary's body dangling from the big trees in the wood. She always cut the body down, but sometimes her knife slit the throat as she did so. Sometimes not, and Mary opened her eyes and spoke. The nightmare had different endings, all forgettable until next time when she suddenly knew she had been here before.

Maggie was one of the first to suspect that Arthur Chamberlain's lessons might have a life in them yet, that the tuition was to be long-enduring. Pandora's box, she thought, once open, never closed. She went on working, seeing Evadne by day, and David at night. John Henry had telephoned to offer sympathy and support. He would not be back: his series looked like a success. His was the one good-luck story of the season.

A week after the cutting down of Mary, Biddy telephoned Maggie at home.

She put her request nervously. 'Would you come to see Mary? She wants to see you. I think she wants to talk to you.'

'I don't know what I could say.'

'Please, Maggie. You need never come again. Never see either of us again.'

'Don't be like that.'

'We shall be leaving the district.'

Subject to whatever happened to Mary, of course.

Biddy would leave Pettit's (she had already resigned), try to get another job (but who would want her); she would find a flat or small house where she could hide with her child. She could see her future, and dreaded it. She had lost everything. She did not blame her child, but she censured herself, accepting all this as a kind of punishment.

'Please, Maggie.'

'Oh, all right.'

Maggie agreed to go, setting a time, but refusing Biddy's company. She did not look forward to seeing the child, but she preferred to be on her own; it must be what both of them wanted.

Biddy was there at the hospital entrance however, watchful if silent. Mary was in a private room. Maggie wondered if there would be a police officer with her, but the child was in bed on her own. A television set was playing at the end of her bed but she seemed to be staring through it, not at it, seeing nothing. She looked up.

'Hello, Mrs Chase.' A small, polite voice. No emotion. Dead.

'Call me Maggie.'

Mary's polite stare did not waver. Names were not on her mind.

'Thank you for coming.' Remember your manners she had been taught, say Please and Thank you. This was one of the habits Pettit's had instilled in her. It overrode other emotions like fear and anxiety.

Maggie had not been so instructed, thus she came to the point. 'Your mother said you wanted to see me?'

Mary struggled upright on her pillows; she looked frail, her skin was very white and transparent so that she could see the veins underneath. There was bruises on her throat but no lacerations. Her eyes fell on Maggie's bandaged wrist.

'I'm sorry you cut your hand.' Polite again, but leaving so many things unsaid. Nor did she really sound sorry.

'Not important.' They studied each other for a moment in silence. She's not a child, thought Maggie, perhaps never has been a child. She has looked into things too deeply, heard and comprehended more than she should have done. No, that couldn't be right, it must always be good to comprehend, what had happened to Mary was that she had seen and got it wrong. 'How are you?'

'Pretty well, thank you. . . . Things to say. To you because my mother won't listen.'

'Ah.' Biddy must be in a state herself.

'She says Rubbish, and not to talk about it. But I must.'

'Go ahead.'

'My mother blames Mr Chamberlain for what happened.' Maggie nodded. 'But it wasn't his fault about Sam, about what happened.'

'No?'

'No. He had to do what he was told.'

'Who told him, Mary?'

'I always knew where *it* came from. Not words. Didn't come in words. Just came into your mind. Sometimes a picture, sometimes just a feeling.'

Maggie knew vividly what she meant: she too had had sometimes pictures, sometimes a feeling. Others also. She blamed this on Arthur Chamberlain, but Mary seemed to be saying that her case and Maggie's were different.

'It was the tree. It all came from the tree. When you went near it then it told you. If you knew it well enough, sometimes you did not need to go near.'

Maggie stared in silence. 'Go on.'

'I first heard it when my father killed himself. I expect the tree told him to, kill yourself, it said, I expect. But that was when I first heard it. It told me not to mind.'

'Trees don't speak.'

'I said talk. You can talk without words. I could talk to you without words.'

Mary fixed her great eyes on Maggie who received such a gust of appalling information about death, destruction and decay that she closed her own eyes tight. Yes you could talk without words.

'Yes, you heard,' said Mary. 'It's not difficult but it doesn't always work. . . . One mustn't rely on it. I could do it to Sam.' At last she had introduced the dangerous name. Maggie opened her eyes at once. Mary had dropped eyes. 'Sam always *heard* me. *Almost* always. He did what I wanted.' Was there a ghost of a trace of satisfaction in her voice? 'So he joined in our game. The pretend games.'

All children have pretend games. Mary and Co had just played theirs with a special force. Surely that had derived from Arthur Chamberlain? Maggie said as much to Mary. Mary said no, not really. Yes, he had made suggestions and talked about *Peter Pan*, but they always talked about *Peter Pan* then, anyway, in her small group. It was what they liked. Their natures were drawn to it.

The tree had already told them it wanted to be played with in that way.

'What?'

Yes, it had told them. As it must have told many earlier generations of boys and girls, to judge by the age of the tree-house.

Everything came from the tree, she said, no point in blaming people. The tree was a story tree.

'Surely not?' said Maggie as gently as she could to the child.

Oh yes, Mary assured her, the tree had what amounted to a mind; it knew a great deal about death, and wanted everyone else to know. Once you had played in the tree you thought of death all the time. Sometimes it seemed a big thing, exciting and terrible, sometimes only a little step of no consequence.

'What am I hearing?' thought Maggie. 'What am I hearing?' A ghost? She said, 'Mary, I don't know what this is all about.' Mary let her know.

It was the tree that had made Mr Chamberlain bad. It was the tree made Sam run away to be a Lost Boy. The tree had told him to come to it. Then the tree told him to fly. Sam had said so. He could speak a bit. More than he always liked to show. That was why he had been on the tape saying his bit. It was a treat for him. He was so proud. Hearing him had frightened the children at the party, but that was because they had never thought he could speak. So Mary told them a witch did it. They didn't like witches. 'Then the twinnies told them that the witch was Ellen. That made them all cry.' And serve them right, her tone said. Maggie could tell she had despised the other children.

'Would they have liked the idea of an active tree better?'

Mary ignored this question. She was beginning to tire and wanted to get on with it. 'When Sam fell out of the tree—'

'Flew out,' corrected Maggie, and then hated herself. 'He thought he could fly, didn't he? That's how he collected so many bruises.' And one day he had flown to his death.

'Flew then, we thought he was dead, so we dragged him away to the little island. But he was not quite dead. It was bad for him, not being one thing or another, so we held things on his nose and mouth till he stopped being alive. ... Then we made him clean and comfy. ... When a person dies, things happen that aren't nice. They dirty themselves. So I got the Flight from the kitchen.' Had she noticed the name of the soap powder? Or was it just one of those dogged coincidences life dealt in? 'The twinnies helped. I could do anything with one of the twins.' And through him, with his brother. 'And Tom – he always *knew*. I never even had to say to him.'

'Didn't anyone see?'

'It was dark. Anyway, they wouldn't have. The tree would have stopped people seeing. It could.'

No answer to that. Not in this world. Or not from Mary.

She was coming to the end, her voice seemed to be getting softer and smaller. 'The tree is a very wicked tree. I see that now. So sad. ... Trees are lovely things, but God made that one bad.'

Maggie saw something was expected. 'What do you want me to do?'

She put her head down on the pillow besides the child's to catch the whisper.

Burn it, came back the answer. Burn. Fire.

She closed her eyes, Maggie watched a vein in her frail neck beating wildly. The little face was sharpened by sickness, the profile pure against the pillow. She looked peaceful. She'd said what she had to say, it was up to Maggie now.

Maggie got away as fast as she could, avoiding Biddy who lay in wait unsuccessfully. Without hesitation she drove to Miss Mackenzie to pour out her story.

Catriona Mackenzie, dragged from the labour of composition, smelt of sweat and scent mingled with the slight touch or two of whisky with which she helped inspiration. The scent was rose-based because the book she was writing was sad, and roses belong to the sadness; the whisky was all her own.

She listened gravely,

'Can it be?' cried Maggie. 'What do you think?'

'Can you curse a fig tree?' she shrugged and laughed. 'Can you put a hex on an oak tree?' Catriona shook her head. 'I don't know if I can come out with you and do any burning.'

'I promised.'

'We'll be seen.' Catriona, now her book was well on the way, had no desire to be in trouble with the police. Art must come first.

'Not if we go at night.'

'We're mad,' she said with resignation.

St Luke is the patron saint of the mad. No one saw them sprinkling the tree with paraffin, then adding burning rolls of paper, but everyone saw the fire that followed.

The big tree smouldered, it burnt blackly giving out a kind of damp heat but no flame. It seemed to Maggie it would never burn. Then a low branch caught alight with a roar, sending out a shower of tiny sparks like flies. Another branch began to burn. The air was full of smoke. Yet the heart of the tree remained obstinately dark, seeming to absorb heat while not taking fire. Patches of grey began to appear on the trunk as if the tree was turning to ash before their eyes. A branch fell to the ground.

Bushes beneath the tree burned so that a circle of fire grew every minute. It had been a dry summer. The fire brigade, busy elsewhere with another fire, was late in coming.

Maggie and Catriona stood looking at their handiwork, for a

brief few minutes before caution hurried them away. 'Come on,' said Catriona. 'We've done enough damage. Let's hop it.'

Maggie lingered till Catriona tugged her away.

'This is where I melt away,' murmured Catriona Mackenzie, looking behind her, as the fire took hold. 'Scarper. I don't mind a little gentle arson all in the way of business, but I don't fancy getting arrested.' She looked admiringly at the blaze. 'It'll make a superb climax to my story. I'm glad you thought of it. Aesthetically, very pleasing. You're a bright girl. A fire is just the thing.'

'It's not a game.'

'No? But Thomas Hardy thought it was a game. The sport of the Immortals, he said. Are you and I the new Immortals? We might be. Lesser gods arranging things to suit our purpose.'

'Is that what you are going to write?'

'I'm trying it out. Or perhaps one of us is the Tess figure: the object of the sport? Toss you for Tess.'

Maggie looked at her, then suddenly laughed.

'That's better now,' said Miss Mackenzie. 'I thought you'd never crack.'

'Well, it was only a short laugh. More of a bark really.'

'Bow-wow. Better than crying.'

The two women went back to Catriona's, because Maggie did not trust herself to stay calm in her own house. 'I shall have to move,' she told herself. 'It's seen too much, that house.'

Catriona made coffee, strengthened with brandy, which the two of them drank thirstily.

'I wonder if we did the right thing? It was madness, really.' Maggie's voice was unsteady.

'You quietened that kid's mind. And who knows? Perhaps we have changed the shape of things to come a little.'

'Why did you join in?'

'Because I'm mad, too.' She pushed the brandy bottle to her friend. 'Drink up.' Maggie drank. 'You know, when we were standing there over the fire we had started, I thought I could smell human flesh burning.'

'If you did, it was yours and mine.'

'Do you mean that?'

'I'm not saying anything supernatural. I have a blister on my legs. What about you?'

'No, it wasn't that sort of smell of burning. Came out of the past, I think. Not real at all.'

'Oh something was burning somewhere all right, but I shouldn't worry about it.' Catriona was cheery.

But, as might have been expected, as may, perhaps, have been intended, her cheerfulness and her matter-of-fact acceptance of the irregularities of life, her apparent pleasure in them, healed.

Beneath the fire the ground grew warm. Deep down in the earth, where the roots of the tree curled around a skeleton, all was cool at first. The heat took time to get there, but it reached the burial place at last. The bones responded to the heat, moving, twisting and turning as if alive again. Heat made the bones roll apart so that the skeletons (there were two, one of an adult, one of an infant) separated as if parting company with each other. The bones could not change colour, the years in the earth had already stained them brown. Some chemical in the soil, a patch of unknown mineral, had painted a darker stain which spread over both skeletons so that even when fallen apart they were related by the stain which was shaped like a large leaf.

As the heat got to them, the bones which had long since been dry, for a second exuded an oily, fleshy smell as if there was life in them yet.

The fire destroyed a large patch of the woodland, leaving behind blackened earth and charred branches. Although the police suspected the fire had been started deliberately, and may even have guessed that it was Maggie, no prosecution was brought. Enough is enough, they seemed to be saying.

No effort was made to replace the tree. The whole area was going to be redeveloped, anyway, as the site for the new hospital.

Before the turn of the century a young boy who was later to be a dentist, and grandfather to Arthur Chamberlain, had walked under the tree thinking about poetry. In those days he had in mind to be a poet.

As a much younger child he once had seen a gypsy woman

give birth beneath that same tree. Before his alarmed but fascinated face, he had seen the child, covered in blood, appear between her legs. He was more startled than frightened, although he recognised it as an occasion for some alarm.

He might have left it there with no bad feeling, if the arrival of a tall adult, his mother he believed looking back, had not turned the episode into one of repulsion. Somehow, his mother's reaction turned everything into bad. For the first time the child felt that adults were hostile and aggressive people who might destroy children if children did not watch out. He never knew what became of the gypsy mother and child, but in his fantasies, both died and were buried in the wood.

This memory was locked in the mind of the lad who would be a poet. Every so often it surfaced, shaping his thoughts in one way and another. He had bad dreams.

As he walked under the tree, worried and distressed by a private grief of his own, a motor-car passed in the road beyond. Inside the car was a small Scotsman who had terrible dreams himself, but who had learnt to put them down on paper and make money by them. Still, there was a price to be paid, and as a child of Calvinism, he knew he would be paying.

These two people never knew each other, just passed once at a distance, but perhaps in the pain of the moment when young Chamberlain was realising he would never be a poet, a maker, their minds met and thoughts passed between them like a bird.

A few years later Sir James Barrie realised *Peter Pan* via The Little White Bird, and Arthur Chamberlain, grandfather, came to Martha Littlebody.

The police saw the whole thing their way; they took their own reasonable, common-sense line.

Sam had wandered out of the house of his own will (whether prompted by another child or not they would never know for sure); he had been able to do this because his mother was a sloppy mother who thought she had locked him in his room while she went to bed with her lover, but who neglected this precaution as she had probably done often enough before. Sam had taken her purse and keys, and good luck to him. The only surprising thing they found there, was that it had not happened before.

The boy Sam had installed himself in the tree-house, been fed by Mary and Tom, and eventually fallen out. They discounted the bird story.

The children, Mary and her group, had been frightened by the fall. But their feelings had been ambivalent, anyway, the police psychologist said. Hate and love well mixed up. A wounded Sam was a victim ready to their hand.

Sam, wounded, had been smothered because his fellows found him 'different', someone who spoiled their peer-group, and whose genes were better out of the way.

He had been killed, probably, by one child. The washing had been done as a ritual binding together in common guilt of the group. It underlined the group guilt. Their psychologist told them there was an expiatory element in the ritual which made them all feel better.

Hard police circles glossed this explanation further. Superintendent Ted Toller believed that the child Mary had killed Sam because she did not want him in her family circle. She saw his death as separating her mother from Nicholas Wylie. She wanted her mother to herself. This was the real story, said Ted Toller.

The police discounted all tales of the influence of Arthur Chamberlain, and still more of Sir James Barrie. Even more so any remoter influences such as that of Martha Littlebody and a malign tree.

This simple police view was now the accepted gospel. Maggie knew well that to the police it was just a straight crime story, nothing else concerned them.

All the fancy bits, the hypnotism tricks, the fantasies of death and blood were just embroidery. The tapes did not prove that the boy Sam had telepathic communication with anyone, or that his mind was possessed by anyone else, it just proved that you should not give kids expensive toys. Autism could work like this; their experts told them it was an inexplicable condition, and it was possible its victims could always perform better than they knew. As for Mary they had known other children like her, although they did not always get away with murder.

And this was the way David saw it too. Maggie knew it would be so. But she came to him the next day and confessed her arson.

He went white with rage and fear, she had never seen him so angry. 'You're a lunatic.'

'I think I am.'

'I blame that Mackenzie woman for encouraging you.'

'Not her fault at all. Please David, try to understand.'

'I understand all right. You've let all this business get on your mind. You must forget it.'

'My horoscope this month is bad.'

'No more of that talk. You promised. We stay in this world. I want you.'

Half crying she said, 'I'm not just the best thing since baked beans.'

What she was trying to say was that she might be a dangerous wife.

He was confident. 'We'll be a team. You're thinking of your first marriage. It won't be like that this time, I promise you. I love you for what you are.' When she did not answer, he went quiet. 'What about you? Don't you like me? Say, and I'll clear out. You need never see me again.'

'You know I like you. Love, I suppose. Yes, I admit it. I never meant to use that word again.'

'Thank you for saying that.' He took her hand. 'Now you only have to say you believe it will work.'

Maggie said, 'Perhaps if we move away from here.' She made it a suggestion.

'No, love, we won't move away. We will live here. I'll join you. Lukesfield suits me. It's a nice place. Besides, you've got a good business going. No, don't let's move.'

He had never been touched by the horrors of Lukesfield. He was too good and, in a way, too simple. Maggie wanted that goodness and simplicity: it warmed her.

They would redecorate the house, she would continue with her job while David pursued his. They would prosper. The

High-Lo cleaning business was doing well; David was quite right, a pity to give it up.

And of course, this marriage would not be like the first one, no two marriages were the same, you made the same mistakes but you made them differently.

No, thought Maggie, we will never move away; I feel it. Somehow I will be here for ever.

She could not evade the feeling that life still had something more in store for her. It had not finished with her yet.

Slowly the affair subsided. Joe said goodbye to Maggie and went off to a new town. He was still a keen believer in a brave Green world but had decided to rest for a bit, and take up photography. He would have to buy a new alarm-clock. He had left the old one behind at Ellen's.

Lukesfield was not to be forgotten, however. A lightly fictionalised account of events was shortly to be published by Catriona Mackenzie. She did not disguise places and characters overmuch, this was not her style. 'People like to read about themselves,' she said. 'They would rather be mentioned than not. And even if they are shy, their friends and relations are passionate to read. The roman à clef is the great genre of our time.' She did not expect to sell the film rights, but she might do well with the book clubs. The libraries she could count on. For her, Lukesfield was money in the bank.

Mary came out of hospital, then was sent for psychiatric treatment in a famous children's clinic in London. Biddy took a flat in London. Pettit's School was closed. Six months later it would open in new hands as a Montessori school.

Maggie and her High-Lo Cleaners had a lot of work so Maggie prospered. Her divorce came through without trouble and she remarried.

Builders with bulldozers and excavators moved into the wood to clear the ground. The day before they went in to start work, Maggie took a valedictory walk.

Where the big tree had stood was a blackened stump. Maggie gave it a kick, and it splintered apart, it was rotten.

But in what had been its shadow two acorns had taken root so that two little oak trees were pushing through the ground.

On impulse Maggie bent down and gave them a pat. 'Be good little trees now. No more trouble.'

Then she remembered what was going to happen tomorrow. It seemed a shame. She took a nail-file out of her handbag, dug them up, and wrapped them in a handkerchief. She put them in her pocket. Tomorrow she would plant them elsewhere. They were good little plants and deserved a future.